Heart of a Girl

Emma Pagano

Olive Tree Books

Chelsea, Michigan

This is a work of fiction. Names, characters, places and incidents either are products of the writer's imagination or are used fictitiously, and any resemblance to actual persons, living or dead, business establishments or locales is entirely coincidental.

Olive Tree Books

an imprint of

El Paso City Books, LLC

P.O. Box 156
Chelsea, Michigan 48118
Ph: (734) 945-2189   Fax: (734) 527-6063

Library of Congress Cataloging-in-Publication Data

Pagano, Emma, 1986-
        [Si accade il 28 gennaio. English]
        Heart of a girl / Emma Pagano.
                p. cm.
        ISBN 0-9729518-1-4 (alk. paper)
        I. Title.
        PQ4916.A35S55 2003
        853'.92--dc22

ISBN 0-9729518-1-4

I hope you dance, little face……

Heart of a Girl

Emma Pagano

It happened 2 January, 1938.

We were all still a little tired from the grand celebration that had taken place during the preceding holiday, and from the lateness of the hour in which we finally slept the night before. It had been such a special occasion, and considering the rarity of days in which we could celebrate in those times, it was worth the small pain to sleep too little for once!

That morning we had much to do – put the house in order, and then go to buy the bread and milk we needed for the day. We lived in a zone by and large away from the centre of town, an area that one could reach only after ten or fifteen minutes walking the grey streets of Paris. It was even raining that morning, but not one of those light fresh rains that lasted only an hour or so; it was truly a downpour that threatened not to leave for at least a good while.

In the end it was Mama' who went to the store, while it was left to me and Francoise, my sister, to clean the remains of the *festa* from the house. There were still plates and glasses on the tables and in corners, and stains and debris a bit of everywhere. But Mama' had always been a very modern mother, and she had immediately liked the idea to invite our nearby English neighbours, Sebastien, Tom and Sarah, to our home to celebrate the New Year, so the fact that the house bore the brunt of it disturbed her very little.

I remember the look, the intensity, of Mama' while she buttoned so carefully her grey wool jacket and wrapped the matching scarf around her collar. Opening the door, that cold strong current of wind forcing itself inside, she turned toward us, looking at us with her grey, girlish eyes, and admonished with a smile:

"My good girls…..make it better please, not worse! I'll be back soon," and so saying, she passed over the threshold of the door and left.

Neither Francoise nor I ever saw her again.

I will never forget her sweet, mischievous eyes that watched over us for so many years, the light in them never spent, not even after the death of Papa' five years ago. God alone knows how she overcame with such courage the death of the man, the one, she loved more than any other in the world, or how, with one look, she resolved the situation for me and Francoise, even as in the depth of her soul she must have suffered so.

It is said that the eyes are the windows of the spirit. For Mama' I think that it was true. It was a quality that Papa' lacked, but he, with his words, could bring you to dream. He was born a poet, and as a poet he died. Lamentably, he found little success when he lived, so often Mama' was obliged to go and work, cleaning the homes of rich ladies in the centre of Paris. I will remember always the courageous way in which she had spoken to us after the death of Papà, a death that she had attributed only to an ugly and mysterious illness... In truth, I had not understood what that strange disease was, and in my still infantile thoughts, I imagined a black cloud entering the body of my father like a halo of ash, blocking the nostrils, closing the ears, filling, suffocating the lungs, dimming, finally blacking out sight. Thinking back now, I know it must have been a cancer, and therefore as a child I did not mistake a lot.

Some days after his death, I asked Francoise where Papà had gone. Crying, my sister told me that I was much too small to understand, but I believe that she had said so only because even she, with her tenth birthday just past, was not certain of the answer either. Then I placed the same question to Mamà. Smiling quietly at me, she crouched down on her heels and taking my hands in hers, warm and soft, she smiled again and said:

"*Tesoro* - Papà told me that God has

called him to come and write a story to read to the angels, as they cannot   sleep in the evenings. Papà did not want to go at first, but then a tiny angel came and prayed him to come. And do you know what your papà said then? He did not become proud, or big-headed or filled with wonder at the divine work that his God had given him to do, but instead said only that he would agree if God promised that he could always be with you. So God gave your dear father great gilded wings, and rendered him invisible, so that he could become our angel caretaker. And so it is now, small one. Papa' is here. He is always beside you, watching over you, but you will not see him, except perhaps as a brilliant, fleeting shadow passing from the corner of your eye."

"But do you not miss him, Mama'?" I asked. She looked at me then with an air of sweet melancholy and resignation, an air that later in my life I would recognize in the security and peace of the most devoted nuns, and said to me:

"Little one, do not worry for me, for I will see your Papa' every evening as I kneel to pray, for the rest of my life, and one day, when I am also called by our God to come and be company to his angels, then we shall be together forever. For now, though, my heart, I must go to work," she finished lightly, eyes glistening, and she stood again.

"Where are you going, Mama'?" I asked in amazement, not knowing that she had taken on work again.

"I am going to help a very, VERY disorganized family put their house in order," she laughed. "Oh, little one, if you could only see the disorder they live with now! Goodness, such dirt there is to clean there, under feet, between their toes," and laughing, she swung me high into the air and tickled me until I could not stop giggling. She was wonderful, laughing and twirling, and I could not see how under it all she suffered so in this reality of hers.

Sometimes I think back again to that period in my life, and each time my mind is filled with one image – always the same…

In my imagination I see a small child…a little girl who has grown too much to wear again her favorite dress. Disconsolate, she tries again and again to get into it, tiring herself out in trying to put her head through the tiny collar, her arms through the tight shoulders, slipping and falling to the floor as she loses her balance. Twisting, trying to hold onto the remains of the dress, she smiles widely before the mirror when finally, with a final valiant attempt, she manages to thread herself into the costume. She is so happy to see the girl in the mirror, dressed so beautifully, perfect in her own eyes, but as she moves to the mirror, hand out to touch her reflection, to caress the velvet in the glass, the dress rips at the seams, falling from her arms to the floor. Nothing but pieces, rags, remain of the beloved gown, and she sits on the pavement, its remnants surrounding her small figure, alone, in nothing but her underslip, and she cries, quiet, invisible tears.

It is this image that I see when I remember that time of my life.

Francoise was just like Mama', both physically and in character, endowed with a strength of spirit and an incomparable beauty. I was more like Papa' – timid and thoughtful. I was always told that I was sweet looking, but no one ever called me a beauty. Francoise was a beauty. Everyone said so. But Francoise was much more …superficial…than I, passing hours in front of the mirror and gossiping with her girlfriends. In the end, it was just a passing stage.

She was fifteen when we lost Mama', while I was not yet twelve. We were so much too young to live on our own, but we were both old enough to understand that in those times of tension and fear, we did not have choices.

I passed the rest of the winter asking myself what had in truth happened to my mother. Often in my fantasies she closed the door behind as she left, without warning finding an old woman outside. I imagined that the old woman, lost, asked my mother where she might find the *latteria* to buy some milk. My mother would, in her kindness, offer to accompany the old one, since she also would go in that direction, but as soon as my Mama' would offer her arm to support the old woman, the old one would grab her by the wrist with long, bony fingers (only the unbridled imagination of a child could conjure such an apparition) and burst into the wicked, terrible laughter of a witch. Then for some uncertain and mysterious - but surely terrible - reason, she would mutter a spell and enchant my mother, dragging her to her underground lair, its doorway hidden under the snow and ice, and lock my Mama' in an iron cage. There my poor mother would discover that the little old woman was in truth a 'troll' who had been about looking for slaves. Naturally my dream always ended when my mother succeeded to escape, and, using astuteness and the force of the right, she would catch the old one with an ingenious trick, and return home, carrying to our house the gold that the old one had stolen. She always shared the gold with the poor neighbors when she returned. These fantasies of mine had taken the place of the stories that I read before falling asleep, and sometimes filled my heart to such a point that I would sleep with the feeling that Mamà was here, seated on the edge of the bed to sing a soft, slow lullaby as she had when I was small and I had fear of the darkness. Sometimes however, these dreams rendered the night frightening and long, filling me with terrible nightmares when I closed my eyes. I saw my mother standing in a cage, her white hands clenched around the iron bars of the prison from which she would never exit, and in my mind I felt her frantic desperation to return to me, to Francoise, and on my skin I felt the scaly hand of the old one...

For the months after, Francoise and I lived in a state of shock – we no longer attended school, we left the house only rarely, we ate only badly. Our behaviour did nothing to diminish the gossip that swirled always about us – at our passage the ladies lowered their voices and whispered conjectures on the disappearance of Mama'. They said that she had run away from us, that she had vanished, that she had died, but none of those was ever sure, and in the long run, our tragedy began to fade from their memory – less so from ours. Our lives were never again as before, but in the agitation of Paris before the second great War, we were certainly not the only ones with problems to overcome.

And so arrived the summer: Francoise was obliged by our economic needs to take on the work of Mama', cleaning houses each day, while I stayed at home only to think and rethink, going over and over again in my mind that day, and what I might have done to avert our loss. If only I had gone that day to the store, if only I had said "No Mama', I will go to buy………", if only I had stopped her at the door……….

The summer was tremendously warm and sultry, and from the roads there seemed to rise a transparent halo of fire. During that time I also took an employment, even though I was always miserable, because even then I understood that it was unjust to leave everything to Francoise. However, this first employment did not last such a long time. I had been taken on by the fabric shop in the quarter to carry the fabrics ordered each day from the warehouse, and to put in order again the pieces that were left disorganized by clients searching through the wares. I managed to move myself for this work only with difficulty, for I was continuously lost in my own thoughts. I managed to maintain my task for the first week. It was in the second week, on an unusually grey and cold morning that I lost control of the situation, and I lost also my position. While I was folding the remnants of cloth, I saw a piece identical to the one from which Mama's coat had been made. The same coat that she wore when that day she was lost to us. Francoise had cleverly, but not without pain, cleared the house of nearly all of those things left behind of Mamà: dresses, objects, cosmetics, photographs. All. It had been easier for me to no longer have to look at those things of hers, things that reminded me continuously of how much I was missing now, and in that small fabric shop I was unprepared to find something so vividly reminiscent of her disappearance.

I was filled with anguish, desperately

saddened at the thought of tossing out that cloth that morning. It was, in fact, one of my responsibilities to toss away the small bits of fabric leftover from the rolls after the bulk was cut away for the clients, into a receptacle for refuse near the back door of the shop. Having seen that piece of cloth, so clearly insignificant yet still terrible in its connection to Mama' and the loss that I wanted to forget forever, I fell to earth, scraping my knees, overwhelmed by an hysterical weeping, clutching it to my chest, that small triangle of wool, but at the same time hating with every molecule the touching of it. I took no notice of anything else until I found myself at home in my bed, the following morning. Francoise had come to take me home after the merchant from the shop had called her, and had been prayed to inform me that they would prefer that I did not return again to my position there. I passed several days of suffering after all, but the shock passed, and I found a new job the following week - a job that paid only half of the first one, but I continued there for the rest of the summer.

Then it was the end of summer.

Francoise wanted to force me to return to school, but I refused to go: my passion for my studies had vanished from my heart with every other emotion but the constant sadness. In the end, the stronger character of Francoise won over my weaker one, and I found myself obliged to awaken every morning and to walk ten minutes to the building where lessons were held, as though I were walking to my own funeral.

At school I hated everything. The schoolgirls who giggled constantly, the mistress who tried so to understand just how terrible my life must be, while the truth was that her constant attention made it even more unbearable, the reading books that told stories of happy children and perfect families that lived in perfect accord.....

I tried to isolate myself from the whole world: I thought that if I could only find a way to forget everything and everyone, then perhaps I would be forgotten also, and I too would pass from this life and this misery. But then I thought of Francoise. Without me, she would be left completely alone, but her spirit would never leave her, and she would die old and alone in her house, even without anyone to mourn for her...........and so I reclaimed my courage, and forced myself to listen to the lessons a bit more each day, and to put more order in the house after school. Overall, it still seemed useless to me – nothing could change the fact the Mama' was no longer, and we were left to administer our lives on our own.

I continued school regardless, and with good results, since even if I did not apply myself particularly, I almost always finished the written tasks without having to study, and in the interrogations the teacher always managed to draw from me the necessary answers. I was weak in my health all that winter though, perhaps because portions were always insufficient in those days, perhaps for the state of depression and solitude in which I kept myself, perhaps from the physical fatigue that resulted from too many sleepless nights that I passed…..perhaps for everything. No matter what the cause, however, it happened that often at school I felt quite badly. I suffered strong headaches, once so strong that my temples pulsed in pain in such a rhythmic sequence that I could barely breathe. Often my knees weakened and I felt faint, and sometimes my vision darkened for a time and I could barely see. I think now that the probable cause of most of these sudden unexpected maladies was truly only psychological, or at the least if really physical, brought on from an event or frustration of psychological base.

Once, during the hour of science, it happened that I fainted at school, and for an instant I thought I must be dead. A moment before I was fantasizing on the eventual return of my mother, with the explanation of the university professor before me entering my poor head in one ear and exiting me from the other. A moment after I felt an atrocious pain in my head, and my vision became darker, and then... total blackness.

It must be like this when you die, I remember thinking clearly, before the blackness overtook everything. Then my senses returned a bit, and without opening my eyes, I heard the voices of the other children around me.

"What is it?" asked one of my companions.

"Nothing, nothing….she only needs a bit of air," my professor, Madame Mercier, responded.

"I'll tell you what it is – I heard my mother talking about her. She has the same illness that her father had, a terrible illness…..absolutely terrible…." It was the voice of Therese DeFroix, the daughter of one of the richest and most socially important families in the whole of the bourgeoisie of Paris.

"*What* illness?" another girl asked curiously, and I could imagine her wide round eyes without even seeing them.

"A terrible thing, truly horrible, something so ugly that you cannot even imagine it. You are *too* young!" The first girl spoke in the tone of one who knows everything. It was also obvious that she knew nothing of what she was saying. "But I can tell you that her mother also had this illness, and it was because of that that she ran away."

"Noooo! My mother told her friends that the mother ran off with a man! A tall, fashionable man – a Spaniard, I think!" and another voice joined, and then the chorus of 'ahhhh', and 'noooo'. It was too much. Opening my eyes and rising, they made a space for me in the center of the circle that had formed about me. Ignoring the words of my professor, the petty comments and giggles of my companions, I walked through the door and returned straight to my home. There, from the anger and indignation (not for me, but for my poor Mama') I gave kicks to everything in my sight, marking the cream colored walls with black from my shoes, and nearly breaking an old antique chair. I thought of the excuses of my professor – she had not *once* proclaimed an idea contrary to the idiocies of her beloved students (she dreamed of being a part of the wealthy circle of mothers that sent their children to her, in the same way that I dreamed of the return of my own mother); neither of us would ever find our dreams, but even knowing that did not serve to make me feel better. I could not banish those words from my mind. I did not wish to, could not bear to think that my Mama' had wanted even for a moment to leave us. No, she could be dead, lost, imprisoned….but if she was gone it could only be for reasons out of her hands, because I knew that she would never have chosen to abandon Francoise and me. Never.

It was not long after that the birthday of Francoise was upon us. Always before I had been happy at the arrival of 23 October, not only because of the celebration and joy that it brought into our home, but also for the arrival of winter that it heralded, and Christmas, and then Easter and after that the summer again. Now though, I could think only that it would be only a few weeks until the anniversary of the loss of my Mama', and the thought frightened me terribly.

This year, we passed Francoise's sixteenth birthday braiding each other's hair and talking of our beautiful life with Mama', dreaming of how

wonderful it would be when we two were able to
pass birthdays and various holidays in a true and
proper family again. And like that, as I twined
Francoise's long blond hair, and she did the same
with mine, dark and waved and so different from
hers, our life together was illuminated for awhile,
and we found in ourselves laughter again, as
though for just a little while the past was gone,
and the future held at bay, and we were gently
closed in a sweet limbo where all was just the
way we wished………..but like all things
beautiful, that precious time too finished, and we
each returned to our proper lives, and my soul
sank again into that abyss of sadness…

And then, that spring, something changed:
for the first time since the death of my Mama', I
made a friend. A true and proper friend who
cared for me, and in whom I could confide my
fears and dreams….. for me, Elodie, as she was
called, was all of this and more. Elodie was
different; though she was born in France, as were

my sister and I, her parents were German. They were not, however, supporters of Hitler and his followers: they were kind to me, and contrary to the ideals of Nazism. Elodie was special also physically: long chestnut hair framed a heart-shaped face from which two sea blue eyes, deep and inquisitive, watched everything about her with curiosity, and a mouth shaped like the half moon, rosy and full, that spilled over into discourses on subjects that varied from her hatred of the colour yellow to the political errors that Hitler was committing, not just for Germany but for Europe as well.

I passed long afternoons with her, lounging on the light blue carpet near my bed to gossip, or, of a Sunday, to stuff ourselves with the tartlets that we bought from Monsieur Blanc, whose shop sat only a short distance from the public gardens where we went to play hide and seek with the other girls. From Monsieur Blanc we stuffed ourselves with sweets, every time buying two apiece and dividing them in half, so that we each had a bite of four different little cakes to enjoy. My preferred ones were the *tiramisù* and the sweet rice cakes, while Elodie took always croissant and the deep chocolate sweets, though the chocolate in particular always seemed to end up less in her stomach and more on her face, especially - and I do not know how she managed to dirty herself so just there - on her nose! Monsieur Blanc was a likeable old man, perhaps a bit too vehement in his patriotic ideas and easy to irritate, but he had a good manner and was enviably honest.

My life was reforming, and even though everything was still a bit confused and disorganized in my mind, I began to feel normal again.

Time passed and soon I would be fourteen myself, and I had begun to conduct myself as had Francoise before the loss of Mama': I sat hour upon hour in front of the mirror, searching for my best features, thinking of dresses and ways to arrange my hair. I had never thought to arrive at this part of my life while everything around me was tragedy, but now I had, and my eyes fell more and more often on the boys of our quarter of the city.

In this way both Elodie and I took a '*cotto*', a crush, on a boy named Antoine, who lived only a few minutes from me. He was sixteen, taller than most of the boys, nearly six feet. When he passed by us he never even greeted us, but we assured each other that it was a sign of embarrassment, as he was obviously enamoured of us....

One day, in fact, we followed him, shadowing his movements like small spies from when we found him drinking at the fountain in the gardens until he returned to his home two hours later. We had such difficulty to keep up with him, running behind him as he rode about on his bicycle, sweating and panting with our tongues hanging from the fatigue; we watched him as he talked with friends his own age, as they enticed him to a game of football - we followed the game ardently from behind the nearby shrubs, now and again letting go an enthusiastic cheer that immediately filled us with a great fear of

being discovered in that embarrassing situation –
we looked him up and down as he stopped his
bicycle to speak to a very attractive girl walking
along the garden pathways – surely his cousin, we
agreed – we followed as he rushed to buy the
things his mother had admonished him to
remember, and as he returned again to his home.
Surely he must have noticed the two girls
following him about all day – one far too skinny,
the other not very beautiful – but in any case he
ignored us completely. We, however, passed the
balance of the week telling each other over and
over again, "And do you remember when he….",
"Yes, yes, and then he…..," "And when he
said…...," "And his friends that……," and "Yes ,
yes, it was SURELY his cousin," "And she
wasn't even exceptionally beautiful…..!"

It was all a game, made of heartthrobs and
dreams, and I wanted it to never end, but too soon
those lighthearted, joyous months were dashed
into a new darkness, a new pain.

It started one Sunday, when, on the streets of the public gardens, we stopped by Monsieur Blanc's. Stepping into his modest shop, into the perfume of newly baked croissant, we felt instantly that something had changed. The low and sturdy figure of the baker stepped closer and closer to us, like the threatening shadow in a childhood nightmare. Stopping less than half a meter away, his small blue eyes narrowed maliciously and his usually gentle voice rolled through the shop like a giant's:

"Get out!" he spat at Elodie.

My dear friend and I stood stupefied by the words from Monsieur Blanc, so much so that neither of us could think or speak.

"Get OUT, I said!" the old man spat again.

"But what have I done?" begged Elodie, in a weak voice.

"I do not want hateful Germans in my bakery!" the man hissed with a threatening air. "So now go, and don't come back," he concluded, and saying so he left us, disappearing into a door that led to the back.

Elodie remained petrified, her eyes bathed in tears, her lower lip trembling violently. When I saw that she did not move, I took her by the wrist and led her from the shop.

"All of those cakes have gone straight to his head!" I whispered, forcing a smile, hoping that a simple strike might repair a little the sweet, destroyed spirit of Elodie, but she crumpled to the ground weeping, and covering her face with her hands, she perched in tears on the steps of a house on the street. I sat down next to her, trying to calm her, but she continued to cry until she hiccupped. After a bit I asked her if it mattered so much to her the opinion of one old man, and she answered me with tears that left streaks down her cheeks:

"This morning the same happened at the bread shop, and also at the *salumiere*. It is all the fault of Hitler, who threatens and threatens, now wanting to invade Czechoslovakia! With all that is blamed on us Germans for the first war, now must come this crazy Hitler to make things even worse. And now Italy, which has become a follower of Germany and quite accepted to form the Axis two years ago! They are all crazy ones here! Don't they understand that we are at the threshold of the 40's now? How can it be there are still so many incivilities after so many years of war and destruction, ending less than twenty years ago? Do they not understand that in the modern society in which we live, the controversies must be resolved with accords and negotiations, not with wars! They are mad…….mad, mad……"

In reality I had also begun to notice the changes in comportment and attitude of everyone around when confronted with Elodie and her family. At school, the girl who sat next to Elodie had changed her desk, using the excuse that the air near the old one was bad….The same professor that had offered me no excuses for my mother, had begun to make mean statements about the Germans, always watching Elodie, but turning always towards my other companions, as if to beg their approval for her comments. Walking through the streets we often found leaflets protesting the actions of the Germans, or sneering and taunting them. Even the headlines of the newspapers, speaking of the menace to Czechoslovakia, was outspoken in condemning the Germans.

By now the cries of Elodie had diminished to soft sobs, and the words that she said echoed in my head. I prayed that all of this terrible story would be finished soon, but already one could hear gentlemen speaking of a new great war that was coming.

Watching my friend sitting there on the stoop, her long hair wet from the tears on her cheeks, I felt an emptiness in my stomach, fed in part probably from hunger, but that seemed to expand inside of me, encompassing all of my body like an invisible tumor, sucking away the joy from the moments of happiness passed with Elodie, and warning me that the tragedies of my life were far from being finished.

Elodie and I were lounging again on the carpet by my bed, trying to avoid any discussions that could refer in some roundabout way to the events of the week before, laughing at anything absurd we could think of, just to keep from saying nothing. Without warning Elodie raised herself up, propping her chin on her elbows, and regarded me directly in the eyes.

"I am leaving," she said decisively.

"What? When? Where will you go? Are you going back to your grandmother?" I asked ingenuously.

"I am going back to Germany," she answered, too quietly. "I will never return."

"But….but….but how? When? With whom?? I beg you, don't go!!" I beseeched.

"In two days I will not be any longer part of your life. My parents have decided to return to Germany, even though they are against the ideas of Nazism that rage there. We cannot stay here any longer – we cannot even buy bread without being treated like beasts, and people that two days ago were our friends now hate us!"

"But I am still your friend, true?"

"Of course, and I will be yours forever, but if you wish me truly well you must understand that I cannot live here. Paris is no longer my home."

I had no words. First Papa', then Mama', and now Elodie. How could it be so unfortunate this life of mine? Knowing not what to say, I threw my arms around Elodie's neck.

"I will miss you till I die," I whispered.

"Until I die…" she repeated.

"I love you well, Elodie…."

There was no response, but I heard the sounds of sobbing, and the thin arms of Elodie tightened more closely around me. We stayed this way for what seemed hours, each crying into the arms of the other.

When it became late, Elodie raised up, her face swollen with tears, and started for the door.

"*Ciao,*" she said softly.

"Elodie, will we never see each other again?" I cried.

"I believe that no one can know," she answered, holding in her hand a scrap of paper on which there was written my address.

"Then how can you say to me only '*ciao*'? This is likely the last time that we will see each other!"

"*Adieu* is an invitation for misfortune. If you say to me '*adieu*', it is as though we know that we will never see each other again. But if you say to me '*ciao*', we can still believe that I have gone only to see my grandmother, and that we will see each other again soon."

I watched her thoughtfully. Could a simple farewell lift the weight of this situation, I wondered? At the moment, it seemed the simplest way to help, so I replied,

"And so '*ciao*', Elodie. I will see you soon."

She smiled at me and left.

The following months I passed hours waiting impatiently for the arrival of a letter from Elodie, but none ever came. My friend had vanished totally, just like Mama', and this time I feared my heart could not bear the hurt.

The summer arrived, and with it many innovations in our lives. The most surprising was the new 'friend' that Francoise had made during the spring. When I saw him the first time I was petrified.

He was tall, blond, tan – he was beautiful. He was also German.

He seemed quite intelligent – he loved books, and in fact had attended the University, but was forced to leave when he transferred to Paris to escape the regime of Hitler.

He hated Hitler.

He hated his politics and his ideas, and hoped one day to return to Germany to help to re-establish a democratic regime and to have revenge on the Fuhrer.

His name was Heinrich, but everyone called him Henri, because such a severe and determined name did not properly fit him. He was very sweet and shy, and he adored my sister.

Francoise said that they were only friends, but I saw the way that they looked at each other. I thought then that they had always been in love, but had just not understood it until that summer. They met in the park, one afternoon in February, and he had offered his umbrella to her, as it had begun to rain furiously. After, he and Francoise became good friends, but when I saw the way in which they denied more, I understood clearly that the case was just the opposite. He could not tear his eyes from her, and she blushed at every compliment from Henri, even those meant only to be an affectionate sign of friendship. One afternoon Henri passed with the two of us, and I immediately found him likeable. He taught to us a bit of the Latin that he had learned at the

University, and I loved this ancient language from the first words. Francoise had some difficulty in understanding it, perhaps because she had always been more skillful in the mathematics, but Henri had rendered even Latin amusing for Francoise, posing questions and telling in the meantime stories of his life at the University. He had also been so kind to me, and perhaps because I was rather timid, he had treated me from the start as a friend. "If you are the sister of Francoise, you must surely be fantastic," he had said, smiling broadly at me, and Francoise, pretending not to listen, had smiled to herself behind her hand.

I remember the evening that Francoise finally realized that she loved Henri. We were clearing the table from dinner, when I asked:

"Does Henri have a special girl?"

"No! He is not with anyone."

"And you?"

"Me? For the love of heaven! Do you not see that I am too busy to think of love?"

"But for Henri you have time."

"But he is particular. He is not interested

in me romantically."

"Are you sure?"

"Yes, yes…..well………no…"

"Are you in love with Henri?"

Raising her eyes from the table in the mischievous way that Mama' had done so often, she said with an intense air, "Perhaps……"

"*Perhaps*? How can you not know if you love someone or not?"

"Oh……. I fear that he does not feel the same way…"

"Henri is *crazy* for you!"

"And what do you know of this?"

"He told me himself," I replied.

"He has? When?" she said, with eyes that shone.

"Ah, well…..he told me not to tell you," I grinned maliciously.

"You would hide something so important from your own sister, blood of your blood?"

"A promise is a promise…" I was enjoying myself greatly.

"I will strangle you!"

"I think that I must take that to be an

admission…"

"It is not true – I do not love Henri. I am only curious!" she excused herself.

"Ahhh... And so I surely cannot tell you! If it were love, it would be one thing, but to betray such a promise for what is only curiosity….?" I replied, enjoying the ease with which I could trick my sister.

"But I love him!"

"AH! I knew it!" I said, laughing and dancing about the house in a dance of victory.

"Tell me what he has said!"

"He has said that you are the most beautiful, the most interesting girl that he has ever met, and he wants never to be apart from you," I told her, thinking to myself that it was not even a small lie, considering how obvious it was that he was smitten with her.

"Oh *Dio*, could it be true? Is it only a dream?" she cried, pinching herself to insure that she was truly awake.

"I think that you should confess your love to him as soon as possible. Tomorrow!"

"No, no…tomorrow I cannot! If I start to

stutter? If I faint? Or worse, if he laughs in my face?" she said, trying all the while to hide the smile that crept unabated over her face.

"Do not worry. He is in love…" I concluded, leaving the kitchen, while Francoise continued to skip and dance about the room.

The next day when I arrived from school, walking into the parlor I saw Henri and Francoise kissing. There was no need to tell me that my plan had worked!

The summer passed slowly, fed by days that we passed laughing with Henri, who, after he and Francoise came together, melted a bit more and began to joke and play with us. Finally we had someone else in common, my sister and I, and he had become an important part of our little 'family'.

To each of us, the months that we passed together were unforgettable, and they helped me to forget the world outside. Sadly, when I began to realize what was happening to France, I realized also that this friendship had blinded me, so much that I did not see that War was bursting around us.

All of the newspapers spoke of it, and the people all said the same. This war would not end. In fact, they had reason to say so – on 1 September, 1939, Germany invaded Poland without declaring war and on the third day of the same month, France and Great Britain declared war on Germany.

Henri had to leave.

His mother lived still in Germany, and he feared that something might happen to her. Even as he loved with all of his heart Francoise, he had to leave her with only the promise that one day he would come back for her.

"Love has no limits," he had said. I watched everything in those last days that we passed together, and I hoped for my sister that all that he had said was true.

I remember perfectly the morning that he

departed. Until that day I had never seen a man weep, but the tears of Henri were so pure and filled with heartache that it seemed to me the most normal part of the world that he wept. It was dawn, and I was there, perched on the threshold of the door, my eyes wet as I watched sadly the farewell between Henri and Francoise. It was then, watching their bodies embrace, that I understood what was the truest love – love was the tears of my friends, that had the good fortune to find each other even if only for a short time. Sighing, I watched while the dark shape of Henri disappeared in the soft rose of the horizon, and crying I prayed within myself that I might too succeed one day in finding that feeling, that sentiment so strong that ties two together and renders them so happy, yet at the same so vulnerable as were Francoise and Henri.

Soon after, letters from Henri began to arrive, but the world continued to worsen and the war continued to grow, always greater and more violent.

"Francoise, get up!"

There was no response.

"Please Francoise, it's seven! Come on – get up!"

Francoise still did not respond.

"Franci, get up immediately if you do not want me to get you up – you know that I will not be gentle!" I threatened as I headed for the bath.

"Fran…." I was interrupted by the sight of my sister sitting on the floor in the bath, her face yellow and her eyes swollen. In the room there was the odour of vomit.

"And so our sleeping beauty is awake!" I teased.

"Good morning to you also, little sister," she replied in a most sarcastic tone.

"I think that I will make a grand breakfast today……..eggs, croissant, jam…….are you hungry, big sister?"

She began to vomit again, and when finally she seemed finished turned to me.

"I feel so badly! It is so strange – I was so well yesterday…"

I ceased the teasing, and helped her to stand, nearly carrying her to the bed.

"Don't worry. Today, rest, and you will see that you feel better soon."

"I…." Not in time to finish the word, she fled to the bath again to be sick.

Sighing, I went to the kitchen, praying that she would be well again soon. Unfortunately, it was not to be, and in the following days, Francoise passed the mornings too ill to stand, and the afternoons eating. One day as I arrived home I found her stretched out upon her bed.

"How do you feel?" I asked her.

"Good, I think…"

"Are you sure? You know that I am beginning to worry for you. It is a week that you are ill this way."

"No, I am fine…..but…"

"Do you want me to call for the doctor? It will cost a bit, but you are in such a poor condition…"

"No. I am not ill in that way."

"Then what is it?"

"I……I.."

"You?"

"I….think…well…I think that I……that I….."

"That you what? Tell me…"

"That I am pregnant," she concluded, wringing her hands.

"P…*pregnant*?"

She nodded her head in confirmation.

"Henri…" she began.

"But you…me….oh *dio*, how will we manage to pay for everything? Who will take care of you and the little one? And if it were to be twins? Or triplets? Or four…..or five……" I succumbed to hysteria quickly.

"I will take care of everything," answered Francoise, now calmer for a moment.

"You will do *everything*? But have you lost your mind? We can barely manage to take care of us…what can we possibly do with a little one to care for in the house?" I had begun to yell.

Francoise began to cry.

"I did not want to …..I do not know what to do…. What we will do….I am sorry….I am so sorry……" She was crying desperately by then, and I, realizing finally that it was even more difficult for her than for me, embraced her and tried to calm her. Holding her in my arms, I watched her with wonder. Was it possible that in that slender, young body a babe was growing? This and a thousand other questions whirled in my head, but all that I could do was stay, seated there on the bed, rocking within my arms my older sister, who now more than ever before had need of me.

The months passed quickly after that. I

took over the position of Francoise, and the idea
of having another person in the house was
beginning to grow in me. I had begun to find
comfort writing verses and poems, or sometimes
even the simplest thoughts. One day, however, as
I returned to the house from working, I found
Francoise running toward me with an envelope in
her hand.

"It is a letter from Henri. I waited for you
to open it – hurry!"

Moved at the thought, I hurried to enter
the house, and slamming the door behind me ran
to the kitchen, where Francoise had taken a seat
at the table and was opening the letter. Peering
over Francoise's shoulder, I began to read the
words written there upon the worn paper.

> *My beloved Francoise,*
> *How are you? I am dying from the need to*
> *see you again. My mother sends you her*
> *dearest greetings. I have told her all*
> *about you, and she has said that I am so*
> *fortunate to have found you, and that I*
> *must not waste more time with an old*

*woman like her when in the end she can
take care of herself. She says that I must
return as soon as possible to Paris, so that
we can be finally reunited.*

*It is misfortune that, as you well know, an
enormous war is building, and I have
decided that I must go first to Berlin to try
to help salvage what small peace there
might still be. Do not worry for me. My
heart is eternally yours. Love has no
limits; even if I must journey for thirty
years to join you again, I will do it, but for
now I must put aside my emotions and
think of what is best for my country and
yours.*

*Give my greetings to your adored sister.
You are always in my thoughts.
With my greatest love,*

Henri

"But he is really a fool!" I cried.

"I hate this! How can you say something
like that? He is a dear! He wants only to save that

small bit of integrity that there is left in Germany."

"He is a fool! How can he think to go to Hitler and say, 'Ah, *ciao*. You know, I think that your political system and your ideas are wrong,' and that he will just *change* them? He must be completely mad! I am the aunt of the son of a crazy man and a fool woman who stands by and listens to him!"

"Stop it! Stop it now!" Francoise was sobbing.

"No – I will not stop. When Papa' died, I was quiet, and when Mama' disappeared I was quiet, and when Elodie went away, I was quiet, and when you told me that you were pregnant, I was quiet still, but now I will stay quiet no longer, and leave that fool to go off to be killed!"

"I know, I know…..but I do not know what to do. I…..I…..I will go to Germany!" Francoise said suddenly, her face lighting up as I watched.

"What? But you are as big a fool as he, then!"

"Did you not read what he wrote there? 'I

will walk for thirty years to be with you again.'
Do you think that I will not do the same for him?"

"But he is not pregnant, and he does not
have a little sister."

"I beg you, help me. I must go to stop
him."

"But are you crazy? Do you know how
long you must walk to arrive in Berlin from
Paris?"

"But it is possible that he has still not left
his mother's home. I might still meet him there!"

"But do you understand that we are in the
midst of a war? How do you expect to cross the
Maginot line? Fly?"

"I will find a way to join him, even if I die
in the trying..."

"Do you understand that you will kill not
only yourself, but also a babe that for six months
has grown inside of you?"

"I have made my decision. I will go
whether you want it or not. Now it is your choice
if you come with me. I was your age when
Mama' died, and I managed both my life and
yours. I am sure that you will be fine if you stay

here alone."

"Are you out of your mind? I could not abandon you, *especially* now."

"Then you are coming?"

"It seems that I have never had another choice!" I replied, and Francoise embraced me, then left to make preparations for our journey.

"Did you bring the blue woolen blanket?"

"Yes!"

"And Mama's grey beret?"

"Yes!"

"And the money?"

"Yes!"

"All of the two hundred sterling?"

"Yeees!"

"Are you sure?"

"I told you yes!"

"Good, then. Did you put the kitchen in order before we left?"

"Yes!"

"Did..."

"*Enough*! That is the twentieth   question

that you have asked since we left the house!" Francoise complained as she walked beside me.

"I know, but I am worried! Please Francoise, let us go back home!"

"It was your decision to come with me!"

"But we have only been walking five minutes, and I feel already a hole in my stomach. It can only mean that something terrible will happen! My stomach is never wrong!"

"Oh no! Run away! The stomach of my sister is saying to escape! *Help*!!"

"What humor, Francoise!" I retorted in the same sarcastic tone that she had used with me first. It was April, 1940. The war was brewing, Francoise was pregnant, and I intended to go to Germany to rescue Henri.

I must have been mad.

It was raining that evening. Francoise and I were sheltering under a tree, because the cost of a room was too great. My sister insisted that we needed to save as much as possible for our arrival in Germany. Instead, I could think of nothing but all of the worries that clamoured in my head, and I found comfort only when I was writing poetry. Francoise was worse, in the last days becoming ill; she had taken on a yellowish colour, she had lost much weight, and her eyes were red and tired. I feared for her health and that of the babe, but she continued to reassure me that all was well, and that her appearance had worsened only from the pregnancy. I was worried for her and knew that if she did not improve soon, she risked losing the child, by this time more than seven months along. That evening, sitting in the shelter of that great oak, Francoise seemed even more skeletal, and the shadows fell back upon her face, drawn from the hollows that had formed in her cheeks and under her eyes.

It was after I fell asleep that it happened. I had always slept lightly, and so I awoke easily from the din made by my sister. I opened my eyes to see the writhing shape of Francoise, lying on the damp ground. I was still a bit drowsy, so I did not understand immediately what was happening.

"Francoise? What are you doing?" I asked her sleepily.

"What does it seem like I am doing? I am …..ahhhhhhh!" she was interrupted by a fit of pain. "*What*? Oh, Saints above us! It cannot be! Not here! Not now! *Dio*, what do I do now?"

"Before anything, calm yourself," answered Francoise patiently.

"But…..but…..what is the first thing to do when someone gives birth? Mmm….and so……you must breathe!"

"That is good…."

"One two……one two…….hmmmm-mmmmm……hmmmm-mmmmm"

"You, meanwhile, give me a clean soft towel…Ahhh!..." another fit of pain.

"Are you well enough?"

"Yes…it is only that the pains come always closer together. You go……ahhhh…"

"I will run!" I cried, overcome with panic. I wanted to scream for help, but we were in open country, and the last house that we had seen earlier that day was more than a forty minute walk.

I bathed a handkerchief with water from the canteen and carried it to Francoise, writhing and crying out from the pain. Placing the cool cloth on her damp forehead I looked closely at her: she was thin, so very thin. It could not be healthy for a woman carrying a child to have so little energy, and I feared that she would not be able to give life to the babe.

At the moment, however, the only consequence that my confused mind could imagine in such a case was that the child would remain inside her forever, and that Francoise would become an old woman of eighty years with an old man of sixty in her stomach. Obviously I was too overcome to realize how ridiculous this was, but this was not my gravest problem that night, as I tried to help in whatever manner I could my sister.

It was near to six in the morning when it finally finished. On the horizon the first light of morning broke, soft and pink in the dawn air, and the countryside resounded with the melodies of morning birds, and with the life that prepared to meet this new day.

But not all was so simple and joyful, and between the trees there rang also the cries of pain from Francoise. She was at her last effort, and the babe ready to arrive, but she was exhausted, devoid completely of energy.

"Come Francoise: the last push!" I urged her.

"I cannot!"

"*Push*!"

"I have no strength left!"

"But you can do it!"

Without warning she locked her eyes on mine with a fire in her eyes, and said to me gravely, "If I bring into this world this creature of mine, I will not live to see it."

"Shhh, do not say such things," I said, but my eyes filled with tears all the same, for suddenly I knew that she was right.

"I am not afraid. I care more for the life of this babe, fruit of my love and Henri's, than my own life. I pray you, take care of him. Promise me...."

"Francoise, stop it! You are not going to die! You are strong...and...and.."

"Promise!" she cried.

"I promise...." I whispered.

She smiled, and watching me, that slender face shining with a kind of golden light in the morning air, said to me:

"I love you, little sister. I will take your best to Mama' and Papa'," and giving one last great push, died, leaving between my outstretched arms a crying babe. I watched this child, and the form of my sister dead before me, and I wept.

From the pain, and the sadness and the loneliness and the joy and the sweetness of this child and the emptiness of my beloved sister.......I wept.

And in the tears, I came to understand just how mysterious and cruel is this life; how there are times that for a spirit and a body it must be paid with another spirit and another body, and how much a creature not even born could be loved, only for that which it represents.

I watched Francoise, who lay on the earth, a smile of blessedness on the cold lips, the pale hands on her stomach, as though to help with the birth of the child. I watched the babe, its tiny body wet still and shaking, the tiny hands clenched into fists that batted the air here and there, and the eyes opening and closing, crying.

And despite myself, I smiled, seeing that he had the eyes of Francoise, but the straight mouth of Henri, and I understood how spectacular was this phenomenon of love, and of birth and of death and of the immortality of Henri and Francoise that enclosed itself in this tiny creature. Covering the babe, I realized that I must give him a name, as Francoise, just past her seventh month of pregnancy, had not thought yet of what to call him.

I knew already his name.

I would have him called Henri, because he, who my sister loved so dearly that she risked her life and death giving light to his son, was a man to remember.

I buried Francoise that evening.

I have never felt a more overwhelming and destructive feeling.

I passed the afternoon to dig the grave, under the oak that was illuminated constantly from the sun. Francoise loved the sun, and it seemed just to me to bury her there. While I dug with a rock that I found there nearby, I prayed that the work would never be finished, in order not to have to cover the body of my sister. But near seven, it was done, and with my throat tight from the golden rays of the sunset, I had to bid my final farewell to my beloved Francoise. I remember that even as I spilled the first handful of earth on her still body, her face held still that peace filled expression, and I could not hold back my tears.

"Goodby Francoise. Do not worry: I will care for Henri. I love you," I whispered, tears overflowing as I gazed upon the heap of earth under which I had buried my sister. Ignoring the earth that clung still to my tired hands, I pushed away my dark hair from my face where the wind had plastered it to my damp skin, leaving streaks of dirt from my fingers. Standing there on the hillside, immersed in the sunset, I could not take my eyes from the grave of Francoise, holding tight against my breast the little Henri, sleeping, knowing that he was everything and all that was left to me then.

I was still stumbling along that rocky road when finally I came upon a small house. It was made of stone, and from the open window floated the perfume of apple cake. I could not stop myself, and I ran to the wooden door, knocking desperately. It had been days that I had eaten little or nothing, trying to satisfy Henri, but the supplies by now were finished. I had decided to return to Paris, and was unaware of how much had happened lately in France.

At the door appeared a woman of about fifty years, a scarf tied about her head and a tender look on her face.

"Can I help you?" she asked me gently, seeing the state that I was in. I could not keep myself any longer on my feet, and I fell into her arms from the grief and the exhaustion, lifted only by the knowledge that finally I had found someone who could help me. Meanwhile she had taken me, held me in her arms, drying with her handkerchief my hysterical tears, and watched with compassion the little one that I held in my arms.

Effectively, I was not exactly in the best of conditions. My blue skirt was torn in places, my hair was disordered and tangled with twigs and leaves, my face was dirty and my hands torn and ruined, and moreover I carried in my arms Henri, a bag of food and a bag of clothes. I looked to be a proper gypsy.

"Excuse me. It is many days that I have been walking, and I was looking for a place where we might pass the night."

"Come, lovely. Be comfortable. You seem to be one who has an interesting story to tell," she said smiling, and leading me inside when my tears had subsided. "Sit, child, and talk, while I make you a nice cup of tea."

I smiled in gratitude, and began to tell of the things that had happened, from the death of my Papa' until my arrival on the threshold of the house of the old woman. She listened to me with interest, once and again pronouncing a word or two of astonishment or compassion. I felt better telling someone everything; it seemed to make my existence more real, the pain more bearable. When I had finished, she asked me, "How long is it that you have not been in Paris?"

"Oh… a long time….." I answered, thinking of it.

"Well, at least you have escaped the German invasion!" she said seriously.

"What?" I asked, suddenly terrified.

"But little one, do you not know that Germany has invaded France? They have taken control and ruined Paris. The soldiers and politicians that were able to escape are all in the southern zone of the country now. It is said that they are organizing a plan to retake our country, but so far nothing has happened. But where have you been until now?"

"Traveling, in the countryside or the woods and small villages. Perhaps I heard things spoken, but was always too tired to realize what was truly happening…." I answered.

"Well, it is best that you stay here with us for a bit….this place is isolated enough that the Germans do not even realize that we are here, and if you return to Paris you could be driven away, or murdered….or worse…."

"I thank you, but……."

"Come and let me introduce you to my husband…" she interrupted.

I followed her into a room that seemed to be a sitting room, where an old man sat in a wine-colored armchair, his eyes shut and a book on his knees, where it appeared to have fallen from his hands as he slept. He was quite thin, and had a few white hairs on a somewhat pointed head, from which sprouted two sail-shaped ears, and a hooked nose. From too-short pants hung two dried out legs on which there sat a pair of ruined old shoes, and from the striped shirt, missing a button, rose two veined and hairy arms. A long hand grew at the end of each. He was truly a strange man, I thought.

"Alfredo, get up!" said the old woman.

"Do you not see that I am reading?" he replied with a rough and strident voice.

"How can you read with your eyes closed?" she asked, pretending to be annoyed, but looking on his face with a hidden smile.

"I am Italian. In *Italia* this is how we read!" he declared with conviction.

"Of course, my love, and in France we speak with our stomachs!" she answered him, smiling.

"You cannot understand how inferior you are to me, old witch," he joked.

"Besides, how can you read without your glasses? You're as blind as a mole!"

"I see you well, my dear – do you not see how young and strong I am?" he retorted, standing. Only then did I realize how tall he was; he must have been over two meters.

" Ahh, ah….don't make me laugh!"

"You are no better, my dear!"

"Ah, but when he was young, he was truly

a handsome man, eh Alfredo?" said the woman, nodding first at me, then at her husband.

"Oh, yes….all of the girls wanted me, but I wanted only Marlen," and smiling he finally noted my presence.

He had a beautiful smile, and gentle eyes, I saw right away. Long straight teeth seemed even whiter against his olive skin, and brilliant green eyes were framed with the longest black lashes I had ever seen on a man. It was not difficult to imagine how handsome he must have been as a young man, and his Mediterranean airs gave him a charm that had not left him, even at this age…..but then neither was Signora Marlen any less arresting, with her penetrating lavender blue eyes, and the fine nose typical of so many French. With the years she had borne a few wrinkles across the forehead, and her black hair was turning grey, but still she bore colour in her cheeks, and her hair and eyes shone.

"Alfredo, this is our guest," she said, presenting me to her husband.

"It is a pleasure, Alfredo DeNeri," he greeted me happily, taking my hand in his.

"A pleasure," I replied in a low voice.

"She will be staying with us for a while," said Marlen.

"Excellent! It is too long that we have no young people in this house!" he announced.

"She has with her also her little nephew, Henri," continued the old woman.

"A babe? Where?" asked Signor DeNeri with pleasure, heading off toward the kitchen.

"He loves children," smiled his wife, watching him with affection. It was obvious even to me that these two still loved each other deeply, but that they were not only lovers, but also friends. I could see it in their words and in the smiles they shared so often.

"Little one! How are you? But look, how beautiful you are!" we could hear the gentle voice of the old man drifting from the bedroom where Henri was sleeping.

"It is such a rarity to find a man who loves children so much, and so openly," I said to the wife.

"He is not only rare – he is special," she smiled, and I could see that she knew what a fortune she had found to have such a man for her husband. We headed together for the bedroom.

With the passing of time, I began to realize just how special Alfredo truly was, and how young he stayed in spirit. I realized too how they reminded me of Henri and Francoise, and though that thought saddened me, still it made my sorrow sweet and easier to carry. Alfredo told me much in those days that I stayed in his home, especially about Italy before the Fascists, and of his youth there. He told me also of his experiences as a soldier during the First World War. He had done his fighting with the Italian Army, but at the same time that Tommaso, his son, was born, he had been wounded in the arm, and so returned to France to meet his new son. Tommaso was killed at sixteen, run down by an automobile. Two days after his funeral, Alfredo and Marlen had moved here, to the country, trying to escape painful memories. But they did not sadden when they spoke of Tommaso, and I often heard them retelling stories:

"Remember the day that Tommy made that castle of sticks and twigs, and then bombarded it with flaming balls of paper? He came home black from the ashes that day!" and they would laugh, remembering with great love, not great pain, their beloved son.

I learned also that before the death of their son, they had been, if not rich, at least very well situated, but they had left behind them everything when they came here, and now they lived on the savings that they had put away when they were young.   Alfredo had been a doctor, and had reached a certain famc in his province.

The days passed in that peaceful way, in that comforting paradise lost in the countryside, isolated from the world, and especially from the war.

Then one day, our precious solitude was shaken.

It was just a normal day. I was helping Marlen to fix her hair. By now, for them I was something of a daughter, and I adored the friendship that had grown between us. I had just started the dinner when we heard knocking. Visitors were rare, and we hurried to open the door, but there when we did was a petrifying sight. There stood two German soldiers, Nazis. They were imposing in their military uniforms decorated with medals covered in the Symbol of Fascism. The one standing in front of me looked at me with cold, threatening eyes:

"Do you have food and a bed for us?" his French accented heavily with German.

"Y..Yes," responded Marlen, frightened.

"We can eat and sleep here tonight?" he asked again, but he knew already the answer.

"Of course, please, come in," said the old woman, indicating the table laid for dinner.

The soldier entered, signaling his companion to follow. The other entering was of obviously a lower rank than the first, and his comportment was much more timid and understated. When I looked up to see his face, our eyes met for the first time, and I nearly gasped from the shock. There in front of me, dressed in the uniform of a Nazi, his hair only a bit longer than the last time I had seen him, stood the love of my sister, the father of my nephew and my dearest friend, Henri.

He was also shaken by our encounter, and immediately he looked at me with eyes filled with curiosity, searching my face to know where was his Francoise, his countenance begging forgiveness for having abandoned us, and understanding for succumbing to the forces of Nazism. Desperately I wanted to say something, of Francoise, or his son, or even myself, but I felt fixed upon me the beastly eyes of the other German. Henri, realizing this also, went obediently to the table where his companion was seated. During the duration of the lunch no one dared breathe, but my eyes fell often to the pale face of Henri, and he watched me with patience.

Meanwhile Marlen worked frantically to satisfy all of the supposed needs of the German soldier. I watched as Henri's light eyes swept the room, searching for any sign of his Francoise. He loved her still. I was sure of it. But she was dead, and I could not bear to think of his heartbreak. I asked myself if he too might die, only from the pain of losing Francoise when he knew. I prayed not.

It was near to three in the morning when Henri arrived by my room. He was even more beautiful under the pale light of the moon. Dressed still in his military uniform, but having left off his hat, he came near to me, his eyes wide with fear of what I might have to say. When, that afternoon, we had secretly set an appointment, I had told him that I had something very important to tell him. Now he watched me closely, his face filled with moonlight, and it seemed as if he knew already the news I had for him.

"What is it? What must you tell me? Where is Francoise?" he begged me in a low voice.

Opening my mouth to answer, the words would not come. What could I tell this man, who had gone against his deepest beliefs for the love of a woman already lost to him? I did not move, my eyes fixed on his face, but my mind whirling desperately, searching for an escape from the harshness of the situation.

"What has happened to Francoise? Answer me!" he ordered, raising his voice in alarm, his hands clenched into fists, not from anger, but from fear of what I might or might not say. Raising his eyes from my bare feet, now tanned from the summer sun, I looked deep into his clear blue eyes and whispered:

"She is dead...."

Then suddenly repenting the coldness with which I had given this saddest news to my dear friend, I flung my arms about his trembling shoulders and clung to him.

Henri did not speak. He did not weep. He did not move.

He stood there as if made from stone, under the weakening light of the moon. His face bent to the earth below, devoid of any expression, but when finally he raised again his face to the moon that overlooked us, watching with mild curiosity this scene with its round white face, one small tear trickled slowly down his face, streaking his cheek with moonlight. That one tear held more pain than the hundred we wept at his leaving, nearly a year before. We stayed there for what must have been an hour, standing one in front of the other, in silence, faces to the ground and minds wandering in our memories.

"How?" he asked me suddenly, his face wrenched in pain.

"She …she was looking for you……..she died on the road…." I stumbled on the words, thinking to myself that it was enough this one terrible surprise tonight, without the birth of little Henri to comprehend also. He had luckily not seen him yet, so there was time.

"She….Where is she…..?" he interrupted. "Where?"

"I buried her beneath an oak tree in the countryside," I said, the harshness of that morning returning.

"Take me there," he said determinedly.

"It is a long walk…..I do not think that we can return by dawn."

"It is not important. Come….take me there.." he said, beginning to walk away from me.

"Very well.......we walk north for a while, then you will see...." I said, breathing deeply. I had no wish to return so soon after Francoise's death to a place so overwhelming, but it was not my choice: in my heart I knew that Henri must say goodby to Francoise, even if it was forever.

During our journey few words passed the lips of Henri, and where before he strode strong and confident to meet the world, now he moved slowly, bent with sadness. I watched him, thousands of questions racing through my head, thousands of confessions torturing my spirit, thousands of confidences and bits of news pinching at my tongue, urging me to speak. Yet all I could force from my mouth was the small question:

"Why are you dressed like this, Henri?"

Henri looked at me, his great eyes glassy and nearly transparent under the feeble light of the moon, so that I thought that if I reached out my hand to touch the light irises, limpid as the waters of a mountain stream, my fingers would sink right down into the light of them. In the shadows it was difficult to see the true colors of the uniform he wore, but there was no mistaking the swastika sewn there, the symbol of death and intolerance, of all that Henri had always hated, but of which somehow he now found himself representative.

He drew a deep, long breath, filling his lungs with the fresh sweet air of the night, and began to speak:

"It is a long story, complicated and long. Since that day when I left you in Paris many things have happened, but I promise you that I have not given up my ideals. I know it must seem that I have fallen under the pressure of Nazism, but it is not so. I would die for that in which I believe – I would so still today – but there has been always something more dear to me than anything else. Something that, even when I was far away and busy with other worries never left my mind or my heart. A worry, a sense of guilt for being away, a sadness......an image stamped eternally on my mind and my heart, from which I can never escape, even if I could choose sometime to abandon it. In truth, I confess with all sincerity that as much as I love my homeland, it is less in my heart than my Francoise, than my need to see her, to know if she is happy, to comfort her in her moments of sadness, to be her dearest friend as she has been for me during long, cold nights hidden clandestinely, a babe lost in the darkness. But it is best if I tell you everything that has passed, in hope that you will see that if I have abandoned my passions and ideals it has only been for a passion greater still…."

I watched Henri as he thrust his hands in his pockets, watching the ground as we walked, and the silence again surrounded us. Silent at length now, I began to doubt if Henri would tell me the story after all, but suddenly he began to speak rapidly, rubbing his forehead as his eyes searched the countryside while he spoke.

"When I left Paris I walked for many days, sleeping under bridges and in the countryside, trying to stay out of sight of the Nazis. After about a week of walking, I came to a small village near Oberstainbach. It had been completely invaded, overrun with enemies, being so near to the border with Germany and I was therefore forced to stay well hidden in the surrounding countryside for several days, always under the threat of discovery by some wandering German squad. It was there, in the countryside around Oberstainbach that I understood for the first time that, without meaning to, I had stumbled into a secret effort, an exercise hidden, badly organized, formed not of soldiers but of common people from the villages and towns, but always an effort of valour and conviction. An effort that I became convinced carried with it salvation. It was the effort, the exercise, for '*Liberta*'. A movement, socially and militarily.......the Resistance.

"And I believed in it.

"The first time that I happened upon these fighters, these exponents of the Resistance, I was hiding in the farmlands surrounding Oberstainbach. They were Frenchmen, plotting an attempt to retake the town from the Nazis entrenched so comfortable there. The fact of my finding these good men was a true bit of fortune for my part, as was my escaping for the most part unharmed from that chance meeting.

"It was afternoon, and I, having heard a rumor from the brush not so far from me, and more than a little afraid of what I might find, managed to pull together my courage and sneak quietly up to the confines of the suspect vegetation. In reality, I do not think that it was so much courage as hunger that drew me close; I hoped desperately to find a hare or even a large lizard, anything that I might have been able to eat. I drew closer slowly, silently, glancing around often in fear of others, but when I saw what was happening behind the brush I let go a yelp of fright! I should never have done so – on impulse, I cried out in my native tongue, in German, and the men that looked up sharply at the noise saw me, dressed in dark colors of the clothing that I had, immediately thought that I was a German soldier! One jumped at me, and then another and another, beating me with sticks and rocks that they picked up from the brush.

"Tu l'as volut! Tu l'as volut, Allemand," they yelled, infuriated.

"Panic stricken, I began to cry out in French, 'No, No, I am not an enemy....I am an enemy of Hitler!'"

"They looked at me, laughing derisively, and continued to beat and pinch me.

"Please," I begged again and again. From the terrible fear of dying there, of never seeing again my Francoise, or you, of losing all that I held so dear, my eyes filled then with tears.....bitter, harsh tears. I feared truly that I had lost everything, and I think it must have been my desperation that caused the three men to believe me, for they paused suddenly.

"You are not a Nazi, German?" one of them asked me.

"I am not....I am not....I swear it!" I babbled, rising to my knees. I felt a sharp pain in my head and down my spine.

"If you are not a Nazi, what are you, boy?"

"I...I am against Hitler!" I cried, uncertain if I had uttered the magic words that would open the door to my freedom or the sentence that would define the road to my death. The three watched me still for a moment, and then two of them began to laugh. The one who had spoken to me extended his large hand, calloused and strong, and helped me to my feet. Nevertheless, I kept my distance, and did not dare to look at them in their faces. All of my bones ached, but I was grateful that they had not killed me. When finally I overcame the fear of another beating, I lifted my eyes and saw that the leader of the three, the one who had helped me up, was smiling at me. His smile was nearly toothless, and the few great teeth that did remain were yellowed and crusted in the remains of the last evening's dinner. His olive skin was scratched above his left eye, and he bore a long white scar from one temple to the other. His meager hair formed a dark halo about his tanned, bald pate, but his black eyes were sharp and brilliant, surrounded by the signs of much sun and labour. He was not a tall man, but very strong. With his hands on his hips, still smiling, he looked again at my distraught face and laughed roughly, turning to his companions and barked,

"He is one of ours. We will carry him to

the base!"

"It was at this base that I would learn to take my part in this secret movement. Of course, they were only a few men worried only for their small town, but from one day to the next I had gone from being alone in this war to being one of a band of brothers of sorts. The leader of this band, as I had suspected, was Pierre, the man who had come to my aid. He was a rough man, jovial and not well educated, but of a good spirit and heart. He had left his family – a wife and four daughters – to come into the countryside and join up with these men, hoping to formulate a plan. Here he had discovered Jean-Paul, a large, hairy man of incredible strength and gentleness. Together they united with Claude and Nicolas, two young brothers who had escaped their hoe to come and defend their county, and finally with a silent, exceptionally intelligent man whose name I have never known with certainty.

"They had already made other incursions against small German squads in the area, managing to kill two soldiers and to wound four others without being discovered or captured. I had been accepted into this band for only a few days when they began to plan their third assault. We united together one evening at dinner to discuss our plan of attack.

"Claude," Pierre chewed enthusiastically, mouth open, on a leg of rabbit that we had captured in one of our traps. "You and Nicolas must hide in the lane that lies parallel to the main road, and when you hear the signal race into the main road and jump on the soldiers you find there. You, Jean-Paul, and you, you……and you!" he exclaimed, indicating the Man with No Name, "you go together and hide yourselves in the brush of the public gardens there nearby. Same story for you: when you hear the signal, rush from your posts and attack the enemy as you find him. The signal shall be a long whistle, followed by a shout…..it will be our battle cry."

"Everyone at the table watched and listened, then nodded their assent, but I was perplexed.

"'And me….?' I asked with some small trepidation.

"You are the most fortunate, son: you will

come with me." Pierre smiled again, then wiping his mouth across his sleeve, he rose from the table. I was trembling, but from excitement or from terror I am still not sure. That evening I did not close my eyes, thinking of tomorrow evening, of the attack, and as always, of Francoise. I passed the following day in a stupor, most likely for my fatigue from the stress and fighting of the day before, but by evening there was reborn in me new my hatred of the soldiers, the Nazis. That evening, as soon as darkness came, we set out in pairs for our assigned destinations. Pierre and I had drawn the most dangerous assignment: we were to secrete ourselves inside one of the shops that had previously lined the main street of the town. Most of these, having been a part of the 'Hebrew quarter' of town, had been sacked and looted; their windows broken, their doors torn from the hinges, they provided very little real shelter, as anyone passing could see easily inside all of them, but we had no other choice.

"We were to wait for the targeted squad to pass by our chosen hiding place. At the end of this road there were several wooden benches, left from the park that had been popular before the occupation, and Pierre, who had been watching the soldiers' movements for the last few evenings, knew that they were in the habit of stopping there for a smoke and a short break. It was there that we were to attack them.

"We reached the chosen shop through a dark and narrow alleyway, entering through the side door so as to avoid the main road altogether. It had been a sort of *salumeria,* selling smoked meats, cheeses and other delicacies. The air was still laden with the smells of salted meats, heavy and inviting, especially to ones as hungry as we were, even as fresh air filled the front of the shop from the broken windows on the street. We sat behind the display cases, alternating the watch on the street outside between us. We spoke quietly after awhile, and in the darkness I could not see the face of Pierre, but I knew that it was twisted from the pain that I could hear in his voice as he spoke of his family. He spoke of them as though they were the world to him, and when I asked him what reason could cause him to leave them when it was clear that he loved them so, he responded simply, "My children must grow in freedom."

"And you, boy? Why have you not chosen to stay in Germany....or with your girl?"

"I did not know what to answer at first, but I thought of his words moments before and agreed quietly, smiling in the shadows,

"All children should grow in freedom."

"I do not know if he saw the pride swell my smile through the shadows, but in one way or another I know that he felt it, and in that quiet night he paid me a simple compliment that caused me great joy:

"You must be a good son......"

"I smiled with pleasure at his words, my cheeks red from the shyness that I suddenly felt, and he knew even in the darkness that he had touched me. Changing the subject quickly, I asked in a voice too strident to be natural,

"You must miss your family....."

"I was much moved by his words, and I felt a great esteem for this man who was so devoted to his wife and daughters. He called them always his 'little ladies' and said that he missed them more than his daily bread. I chuckled with him in the darkness as he recounted many of those small things, those that seemed so important on that melancholy night. I held my hand to him when he confessed that he feared more than anything never to see them again.

"My little ladies," he said, his throat close and his voice raspy, "What could I do without them?"

"I did not know how to comfort him, but had I found even the perfect words there would have been no time for them. In that moment we heard the voices of approaching soldiers, laughing and talking boistcrously as they walked. They passed their lanterns and torches into every dark angle of the street as they came, through the great shattered windows of the ruined shops, into the small panes of the homes along the roadway. As they passed the *salumeria* where we crouched, the torchlight blazed only millimeters from our hiding place beneath the counter. I could feel my heart lodged in my throat. The soldiers, however, unaware of our presence, continued on down the road after a moment, and Pierre and I hurried to follow them, watching their movements closely from behind.

"Finally they arrived at the benches that marked the old gardens, and for a moment I feared that they would chose this night of all to renounce their evening smoke and continue on their way without stopping, while some small part of me hoped at the same time that they would in fact do just that - keep walking and talking and laughing, further and further until our plan would be aborted. My doubts evaporated quickly as I watched one of the men extract from his pocket a packet of cigarettes and pass it among his fellow soldiers, all the while continuing their conversation.

"When we were certain that the German squad was absorbed in their break, we prepared to attack, and Pierre, placing two meaty fingers between his chapped and ragged lips let go a long, shrill whistle, followed quickly by a grand shout in his strongest voice. He launched himself into the midst of the soldiers, shooting off an old pistol and hitting one of the soldiers, who fell to the ground, dead. I followed him, throwing rocks and hitting the incredulous men with a great stick that I had found. The soldiers spat profanities in German into the air around us as others of our band revealed themselves and rushed into the fray.

"I know that I was beaten many times, and I remember hearing shots all around me, but the truth is that in those moments I was conscious of little. I was completely, inextricably immersed in a sea of hatred, and I struck the soldier nearest to me with a fury that brought him to his knees on the earth before me. I thought nothing, feeling only the adrenalin rushing to my head, and I exulted inside at the thought that I was winning this confrontation.

"When finally I realized that it was useless to keep battering this dead man, I looked about me, wild-eyed and frantic, spit and sweat dripping from my mouth and chin. But all was not as I hoped.

"No.......it was just the opposite. It was true that the Nazis had suffered, all down, either dead or soon to be, but we were also sorely broken, and Pierre and Claude lay dead.

"This attack, this fight, had not been as I

had imagined the night before. In my foolish mind I had dreamed that all would go well, that we would fight valiantly and finish victorious, that I might become a hero of sorts, but when I found before my eyes the bodies of my two new companions, I was destroyed. Strangely, I shed not a single tear from my exhausted eyes, nor could I begin to console Nicolas, who wept disconsolately at the death of his brother. Frozen there, immobile, horribly fascinated by the sight of those men who had died for their ideals, ideals so seemingly unreachable, I was overwhelmed by images of the past days whirling through my mind. When finally I tore my eyes from that atrocious scene I realized that I had begun to hum an old song, popular years before.

"It was the 'Man with No Name' who called me back, pulling me by the hand and urging me to escape, to flee with the few remaining. I looked over at the men retreating from the sight of this small battle, again seeking refuge among the farms and woods outside of town. Before my eyes I counted three, men whose lives had changed, broken and destroyed by this war. Jean-Claude carried Nicolas away over his shoulder, Nicolas kicking and struggling to free himself to return to the side of his dead brother. His tears frightened me, overcame me and forced me to understand finally that I could not stay there. I could not continue to fight this way, in these small personal efforts that tore my heart apart. This horror needed killing at its heart, and I knew that only in that effort could I find some resolution of this conflict in my heart. I watched the three men leave, listening to the last cries of Nicolas fade into the night, and when finally again there was silence I knelt by the lifeless bodies of these brothers and closed their eyes one last time, eyes still wide with the fury of the fight.

"Poor Pierre, I thought. *He knew…..never again to see his wife…..his daughters….or them him…*

"That night I left that place, traveling in the opposite direction of my ex-companions, working my way again north, nearer and nearer to the border. I wandered for days and days, eating rarely, drinking only when I had desperate need. I passed kilometers and kilometers, wishing all the while that I could close myself off in some dark, quiet cave, alone to lose myself in thoughts of what I had lost, what I had seen others lose.

"Then I thought of Francoise. I saw before me her face, her expression calm, her way gentle and sweet as when she would take my hand when we walked together. I thought of her constantly; dreamed of her at night. No…. in reality I did not so much dream of her as awaken in the morning with the sensation that she had passed the night by my side. The only dream of which I was sure, I could never forget. In truth, it was a dream that came to me nearly a year after I left Paris.

"In the dream I walked alone along a lane in the countryside, on a day hot and heavy with humidity, and the salted tears that streaked my face melded with droplets of sweat that rolled from my temples, dark from the sun. I cried disconsolately, desperately, as I have never cried before, but when I awoke I could not understand why from the memory of this vision. In the dream, suddenly before me on this lane I saw Francoise, walking along the opposite side of the road from me. I smiled and called to her, and she passed in front of me, fixing me with her eyes as she neared, saying nothing. Only at the last moment did she reach out to me, her hands pale, her fingers long and slender. Our hands brushed gently, lightly together.

"Her face was creased into an expression of fatigue, of great, exhausting concentration, as though she required tremendous force to reach out to me, but when she looked at me, she smiled. Then it was done, finished, and in a matter of an instant she was again gone. But even now, when I close my eyes I see her form before me again, slight, pale, dressed in something filmy and white….and I see again her skin, nearly translucent, her light eyes at the same time lighthearted and melancholy, her smile sweet. I have never forgotten her, I promise you, little one," he said, looking at me with tears in his eyes. "I have never forgotten…….."

Henri walked on in the night, the land about us picturesque as the drawings in a child's storybook. Around us swelled the songs of the insects and the sounds of the country, and above us the starry night sky mirrored the multitude of fireflies that danced in the grasses of that immense territory, and I thought again of the eyes of Francoise, shining in that same manner. I asked myself if it were possible……if……if Francoise had desired so much to see Henri that she truly came to him in his dream; and while my mind remained still and quiet, not daring to answer, my heart beat wildly and I knew with certainty that in that precise instant in that strange night, Henri had not only dreamed of Francoise: he had touched her…..felt her…..and she had summoned all of her strength to go to him for that last farewell. My sister had bid *addiu*'….no…*arrevederci,* until we see again the other…….to Henri there on that roadway, traversing the barrier between life and death and all that lies between, and she had touched for an instant. I wanted to weep, but not from sadness: from sentiment, because I knew that regardless of the war, the times, her death itself that divided them so surely, they would be always together.

Beneath my tears I smiled, and in that moment I understood that Francoise walked nearby even then, smiling at the clarity of Henri's love for her, knowing how he had always loved her.

Timidly I held out my hand towards this man of Germany, and he took it for a moment and held it sweetly. He smiled at me then, a smile filled with gratitude and suffering, and then lowered his eyes again to the dusty ground, rising beneath our feet as the road began to climb.

I was curious to hear how his story continued, but I was afraid that Henri might not speak again about it. I knew that the telling was painful for him, the memories difficult for the sadness that they carried with them, and so I could not ask him to go on: I waited for him to speak of his own accord, breathing in only the silence of those seconds of indecision, until finally, almost in a whisper, I heard his voice, and I moved closer to him to hear.

"Soon after, I reached the town closest to

the border with Germany, and I stayed there for
several days, resting in the surrounding
countryside as much as I was able, having always
to stay on the alert for fear of being discovered by
one of the many squads that passed through the
area. I saw much in those days. Men – tall,
young, strong, men with muscular limbs and
powerful hands, inexpert but cruel. I watched
them from my hiding places as they practiced
their aim, using as their targets the branches of
the old trees there, branches that fell often to the
ground amid a shower of leaves and dust; after
awhile they discovered that it was more
entertaining to shoot at the rabbits and other small
animals that abounded in the woods there. I
looked upon them as a child looks upon a great
painting: I saw them as beautiful and yet
incomprehensible, and I found at the same time
disgust for them and for their behaviour, and a
remote sense of jealousy. Jealousy of those
bastards…..they were not obliged to lose those
dear to them, to hide themselves in the
countryside as criminals might; jealous that they
were lighthearted and well; jealous that they had

no doubts of that great power called Nazism. I envied them, in fact, even for their absence of understanding of the atrocities of the government and the Movement in Germany and in Europe, their ignorance in not seeing that which I had seen. I wanted also to gain inspiration from a force greater than myself, to have someone to idolize, to believe in, to take pride in his position as a leader of my country. And I admit to you now, little one, in all sincerity, that I have tried sometimes, when I awake alone in the middle of the night, shoulders and back aching from sleeping on the ground, arms covered in insect bites. I have tried to imagine myself in that uniform, dressed as one of them, happy in my ignorance, thoughtless of the world about me………I could not do it. I could never see it, I swear…..and that is the reality.

"I saw them once, after this, shooting at a stray dog that wandered near to them, wagging his tail and begging for attention, and all of the hate that I had felt before for these men came rushing back to me. I had to force myself not to launch myself against them every time that I saw them. Their laughter echoed in my head, the sounds of their shooting, the whimpering of the poor dog that lay dying from their games. My nose was filled with the pungent smell of the gunpowder, of the grass, of the canine's blood that dyed the vegetation where he lay. My eyes were flooded with visions I could not escape: Pierre, my friend, that dog… in my mind their bodies fused together and fell simultaneously on the grass, wounded, dead.

"The dog had died too, under the dispassionate eyes of the soldiers who had made bets on the length of time the animal would struggle before finally succumbing to its inevitable death. I had forced myself to stay still where I was, though the dog's cries and the German's voices were driving me mad.

"When they had finally left (the tallest man had won the bet: the dog had died from blood loss in the range of twenty minutes), I sat near the animal's quiet body. The light fur seemed stained by rust, the beautiful face was covered in spittle, the strong throat had been pierced by a single bullet, but it had caused a great blood flow. The glassy eyes of the corpse were turned towards the sky, pleading, perhaps sending a silent prayer to his killers. Help me, please.

"I dragged the poor dog under a tree, where his body would be sheltered from the sun, and I quickly ran away, my eyes damp with tears. Only when I finally stopped, sweaty and breathless, did I realize the risk I had taken in moving so openly, and I immediately searched for a new hiding place in the high grass. I never returned again to that area, disgusted by the idea of coming across the putrescent carcass of the dog I had seen die."

"So then? Where did you go?" I questioned, not managing to reign in my curiosity. Henri breathed deeply and continued, shaking his head.

"Even if I had wanted to move on, I could not have, not even if I could have wished it so."

"Why? Were you hurt? Did you get lost? What happened?" I asked, my voice trembling like that of a little girl.

"No, little one….worse…." he smiled wanly. "… I went to town one day, planning to camouflage myself in the midst of the townspeople. It was a Sunday, and there was a fair, as I had found out by listening to some farmer's conversation. I had an immense desire to stay in the company of people, if only for an hour. It didn't matter, even if it was for only a short while: I needed desperately to know for a bit that I wasn't so alone.

"I feared I was going mad, that I was becoming a mere spectator of the lives of other people.

"And so I entered the town, a small, charming town, made up mostly of farmers and shopkeepers, of uneducated people that had accepted without much conflict the Nazi invasion. In that moment though, I didn't care. All that mattered was that they were people…I would not be alone…

"I walked around the *fiera* stands, tasting all that was offered freely, suddenly remembering how good were certain foods I had forgotten, in the time since I had left home. I tasted desserts, bread, fried foods, vegetables. I was highly satisfied of my visit in this town, until something that should never have occurred actually happened unexpectedly. I suddenly heard the ringing of car horns, and saw the crowd parting diligently, between whispers and loud exclamations.

"I saw a black car – how long it had been since I'd seen a car! It was shiny, expensive. On the back a Nazi flag danced in the breeze, and from the rear seats, a short, round, balding man in a Nazi uniform was nodding to the people around him. At his passage everyone raised their right arm, their fingers pointing skyward, and many were yelling words of welcome or support.

"He must have been a Nazi general of some sort, or at the least some ranked official….. I'm not sure. All I am sure of is that I watched the scene without moving, frozen by the disgust I felt, and then turned to run away, as far away as possible.

"I dodged and squeezed between the happy, enthusiastic people, finally extricating myself at the far end of the stony road, and I began running towards the lateral roads that lead outside town. Overhead, the sun shone strongly, blinding me and giving me an aching head. Suddenly I ran straight against something. Or rather I should say, against someone.

"For an instant all I saw before me was darkness, but then I felt a hard, strong hand grab me.

"What are you doing, idiot?" a voice, heavily accented with German, asked coldly. "You do not salute he who is more brave than you? You do not love our superior? You French beast, I order you to salute that man, I order you to hail, 'long live Hitler', to kneel down before me!" barked the man, his clear blue eyes gleaming with hate.

"No, no, no…." I babbled rhythmically. I did not understand well what was going on around me anymore, my head throbbing furiously. All I really knew suddenly was that I would never back down from my ideals….not for this breed of animal. I preferred death.

"No? No? I order you - do it now!" he yelled again, as small drops of his saliva covered my face.

"No." I repeated, freeing myself forcefully from his grip.

"Suddenly he hit me, and I fell to the ground. I'm not sure of all that happened… I do not remember all….. I thought I was dead, or dying……. the only pain I could feel, even as his heavy, boot-clad feet descended on my body, kicking me with anger, with incredible fury, was the steady pounding in my temples.

"I remember then hearing a German voice yelling "Alt", saying something about how they would 'send me'… I could understand little and nothing, and the last thing I remember was the great hand that pulled me up, and the feeling of a gun jammed into my back as I stumbled roughly through one of the smaller streets. I recall a truck, and many tired and angry faces, and that I was forced onto the truck with these other men. The rest is darkness in my mind.

"When I awoke in the stench of urine and sweat, the light brightly invaded my eyes, bringing back the headache I had forgotten. I suddenly vomited all I had eaten, drenching myself and shaking. I looked around and saw those other men, most of them in the same state.

"Who are you?" I asked, my breath coming raggedly.

"We? We are part of the Resistance," scowled one man, his skin black with dirt. He began laughing, quietly at first, then more and more hysterically, throwing his head backwards. The other men chimed in, cackling in the same horrible way, and the fear built inside of me.

"Where are we going?" I asked, fearing the answer.

"*Lager*.......the camps......"

"I fainted again.

"When I awoke, night had fallen. Around me hollow faces stared through each other. No one slept. In my head a voice, like nails screeching on a chalkboard, screamed continuously:

> *LagerLagerLagerLagerLagerLagerLager*
> *LagrLagrLagrLagrLagrLgrLgrLgrLgrLgr*
> *Lgrlgrlgrlgrlgr...*

"Suddenly, desperately, propelled by the terrible fear inside of me and some deep instinct of survival that lay still in the heart of me, I threw myself towards the back of the truck, leaping out towards the road in one wild movement. I flew five or six meters from the still moving truck, landing further because of the steep inclination of the road that we had just covered, and rolled backwards, bumping and beating myself upon the rocks as I lost myself in the drop and the hillside, sure that I would die, and then again came darkness before me.

"In truth, I had only fainted, as before, and I awoke to find myself at the bottom of a steep gully, lying in a bog of mud and dead leaves. I was covered in mud, leaves and black muck. I tried cautiously to move, but I hurt in every bone and muscle; still, I seemed intact, nothing broken and all still able to move and bend. I stayed there, stretched out in the mud and muck, contemplating the sky above me, framed so delicately by the limbs of tall trees and their leaves, and I began to laugh and cry at the same time. Laughing for the wild escape from certain death in *Lager,* the concentration camps of the Nazis, crying for the knowledge, the realization, that all of my hope was for nothing. I was a man alone, and sure that I would soon come upon another opportunity to be captured and sent off to my death. In that moment, half-buried in the mud, I came to a decision. But before anything else, I had to insure that my mother was safe and well.

"When I had recovered enough that I could find again the strength and the desire to move from that place, I stood, exhausted, lifting myself from the muck, and I pulled off the clothes that I wore, covered in mud, wet and heavy. I stood nude in the middle of the woods there, and hung the clothes as best I could on the trees and bushes to dry out. As I worked, it crossed my mind to look for an instant in the dark mirror of the bogwater, and as I did so I was dumbfounded. I seemed another man. No longer did I wear the countenance of a young man, healthy and strong….I was transformed into an old, broken man, a sack of sharp bones covered with skin…I could count the ribs that appeared in the mirror, my cheekbones sunken beneath my eyes, my kneecaps protruded from my legs like nails from a wall. I was pale, dirty, covered in bruises……I wanted to cry, but tears would not come from my eyes. I touched my face. I had never been inclined to wear a beard, being not so hairy by nature, but from my face now there grew a light fur, and my blond hair brushed my shoulders. I seemed an old stray….."

"But where were you by then?" I asked Henri, breaking the spell of that image frozen in my mind, that he had described so clearly.

"This I discovered when I happened upon the nearest town in that countryside. First I walked for some hours in the woods and bogs, as I found myself in a zone with few habitants….it was fortunate for me, for if it had been different I would have likely been recaptured by soldiers quickly. I came upon the town at night, and it was almost delicious to see the houses, styled in the German style, all much the same, and I was overcome with a wave of nostalgia that filled my spirit. It was almost immediately overtaken, however, by a sense of desolation, when I came upon the Hebrew quarter, that had been completely destroyed. On the walls there were Nazi slogans and posters with images of strong, proud soldiers, or Hitler himself, in some noble pose or other.

"I hid myself still in the countryside until dawn, until I began to see movement on the road, and then I entered the town , staying only long enough to ask what place this might be. I asked information from an old woman who was sweeping the ground before her house, and the old one, without even raising her head, answered me roughly:

"Shönau, fool!"

"It surprised me to find that I had lost the habit of speaking German, and the words were difficult to force fluently from my lips. But it surprised me even more to realize that the town in which I found myself was not so far distant from my home. Immediately, I took to my feet, traveling in the direction that I believed to be correct, and bit by bit, as I neared the town where I was born and had grown, I began to recognize signs and details of the road. I still walked two days to arrive, and when finally I set my feet upon the streets of my home, I was exhausted from the pace which I had set from myself, but I was still anxious to find the road to my own home.

"As I walked the streets of my home, I was saddened to see houses demolished, streets dirty and filled with holes and debris, flyers nailed to every surface. I walked along the grey streets, remembering with nostalgia all of the places that were dear to me as a child.......the fountain where I drank with my friends after the hundredth game of hide-and-seek.....the school where I passed happy hours immersed in the world of knowledge and learning......the public gardens, in ruins now, where I rode my bicycle with my companions on hot summer afternoons.....It seemed that someone had taken my memories and changed them all.....nothing was as it had been. I saw sadness, desolation, fatigue everywhere. I thought of my old friends, my companions, probably all now become diligent Nazi soldiers. I thought of my Hebrew friends, wondering if they were all now dead. I tried to force myself not to see, walking quickly to pass the last bit of road before arriving at the house where I had lived. I walked with my head down, thinking of how many times I had passed that road before, from the time when I was small, until I lifted my eyes, and……..the little white house (demolished, destroyed….), the brilliant flowers (burnt to ashes, dead….), the little stone path (torn apart, buried….), the good smell of chocolate cake (the odor of death, of ashes and flames…..), my dear mother that smiled at me from the window and came to hug me at the doorway (where was my mother…….where?…..) I retreated, bumping into a passerby. I turned and recognized the old postman, but he did not know me, and I thought it best not to alter the situation. With my voice trembling I asked:

"What has happened to this house?"

"He shook his head, covered in thinning white hair, and he peered at me through green eyes framed by countless deep folds: "A bomb, son. An English bomb."

"*A bomb..a bomb a bomb bomb*……….

"And the people who lived here….?" I asked, but regretted it right away. "No, wait….please do not tell me…..I beg you….” I spoke quickly, dropping my eyes to hide the tears from the gaze of the old man. I did not want, could not bear, to know. Whatever the answer, it would torment me for all of my life, and I could not bring myself to do what I knew that I would have to.”

"What do you mean?" I asked Henri, not understanding right away.

"I had done the only task that remained for me to do. I turned, putting my back to the old postman and the house of my childhood, destroyed and forgotten, and I departed for the last time. Suddenly I heard a voice behind me, uncertain, inquiring tentatively: "Henri?", but I did not turn. It was the voice of the postman, but to my ears it was the voice of the house, that had recognized me and that I had now to forget forever.

"I hid in the countryside for the following days.

"I ate anything that I could find, washing myself in a cool stream. I did everything that I could to make myself presentable. I am sorry to admit it, little one, but I stole also. I needed badly to find some clothing to wear, as mine were terribly torn and filthy, so I took what I needed from the house of a man in the night. I did not know him, and I think that if I had I would feel even more guilty for my theft. I try to imagine that he was most likely a Nazi official, but I cannot, for I know that it is not true, and that even if it were, my behaviour would still have been wrong…..but it was necessary. The next day I presented myself at the headquarters of the Nazi contingent in town, and declared my desire to become a soldier," he explained, and his voice was broken by tears and hiccups.

"I understand, Henri….you had no alternative….." I tried to comfort him.

"No, I had done something very wrong, and it is worse that for this I find myself here now. The soldiers asked me many things, including why I had waited so long to enlist. I made the excuse that I had been traveling, but that now I was available and prepared to give assistance to my country. My lips seemed to burn and my tongue to twist in my mouth when I uttered these false words, but they were necessary. I told them that I wanted to go to France, for my dream was to aid the unification of Europe under the banner and power of Hitler, and they believed me. After a short time, probably because of my capacity with the language, I was assigned to a group of soldiers headed directly to Paris. Journeying with them, the trip was much less difficult and adventurous, but more painful for me. I swear to you, though, that not once did I kill a man in the name of Nazism, on all of that long journey. I became one of the more appreciated soldiers of the squad, valued by the general for my strong sense of orientation, and it fell to me often to plot the most favorable roads for our travel. The maps were consigned to me, as well as a title bestowed in jovial envy by the other soldiers – 'Compasshead.'

"No, I did not have a great rapport with the other young men of the squad…they recognized something in me that was different, as dogs are able to sense in the air the odor of a cat, and as I preferred not to abandon totally my principles and ideals, I found it difficult to lick the boots of these assassins. Never…..

"All the same, as I have already explained, I had become a favorite of the commander of the squad, and he included me in his decisions, asking for information and my perspective when he evaluated his movements. He told me often that I was the sole member of the squad who seemed capable of reasoning in a sensible manner……if he had only known……

"It was for this strange rapport with the commander that I came to be here in this area now. Yes, my dear, that man with whom I arrived is a Nazi, and he believes absolutely that I follow the party line. We had gone ahead to try to find a shorter route to Paris. We must return to the encampment where we have left the remainder of the squad, to provide information on the countryside that we have discovered, but now……Now we have found each other again, and every fiber of my being screams *'Donotgobackdonotgobackdonotgobackdonotgob ack'*, in a single, overwhelmimg voice."

I looked at him, and it seemed truly that

he tried desperately to contain that terrible screaming in his soul...knuckles white from the physical force that he spent there; hands pressing against his temples so forcefully that he carried the expression of one who had seen a hundred years; lips bitten and tight from the strain of his emotion: pain, hate, fear, desperation.... But in the same moments, in his eyes, that under the caress of that soft moonlight silvered and softened, I recognized the same veil of hope that he had in his eyes when he left Paris for Germany, determined to change the world. Now, he had seen that the world did not change so easily, but as he remembered all that he had left behind him, all which awaited his return, the memory of it all was sweeter than any dream that he might have dreamed.

Now my entire body trembled, not on the outside, but inside me, at the thought that tonight I must show to this man the tomb of my sister, that in recounting to him the manner of her death, that I had seen, had sealed the death of his soul....No, I could not bear to think of it.........

But I had had no choice.

I could not imagine what Henri needed to do in that moment, having relived the pain and desperation of his terrible journey, only to return to find his beloved Francoise was no longer with us. Here in this place, on that hillside, we knew then that Francoise was no longer in a different state, but transformed. Gone from our lives as the spring breeze that suffocates in the sultriness of summer, taking with it the soft perfumes of the flowers and the beauty of the spring meadows, but leaving alive in us all the memories.

They must have been all around us when

we arrived there at the hillside. Walking on the
fresh earth, I could almost feel the vibrations,
pulsing from under my tired feet, as though
Francoise, spirit, ghost or angel that she might be,
was greeting me. The tremors, the vibrations
underneath me seemed almost still when Henri
came close, as though trying to hide the sorrow
they contained to have lost him. Henri walked
slowly to the mound of earth, covered with
flowers that by now were brown and dried under
the sun that lay always under the beech. He
watched as a wave of grief passed through me,
bringing me to silent tears. Henri stayed there,
standing before the 'tomb' that I had dug, his
eyes wet with tears and his legs trembling.
Around us the sun began to rise, rose-colored and
pearly like that morning, months before, in which
I said farewell to my sister, wrapped in the
lukewarm dawn. Now though, it was Henri who
wept, a light breeze tugging gently at his blond
hair. The countryside began slowly to awaken,
and soon we found ourselves immersed in the
endless sounds of morning birds and animals. I
stayed there to think, sitting on a stone not far

from the beech, my mind captured by the sadness and the memories.

Returning to the house, I thought of how much shorter the journey when the march was constant, and without the weight of bags and children. As we walked, Henri and I began to talk. We spoke of all of the things that had happened in this year, of what we each had done, of whom we had met.....and suddenly I realized that I still had not spoken of little Henri, and that, as Henri himself seemed to have recovered a bit from his previous shock, I decided to tell him the rest.

"Henri, there is more that I must tell you, something that I have left out of the telling of the death of Francoise. .." I said, walking uncertainly beside him.

Henri stopped in front of me with a questioning air.

"You remember that I told you that she weakened and died, looking for you, I did not say, but I knew, the true cause of her death.....you see....she died...." I said with despair, "she died giving life to your son. You are a father, Henri," I finished, smiling tentatively, hoping to lighten a bit the surprise.

Henri stood paralyzed, but a light shone from his swollen eyes.

"He is your son, Henri. Francoise was searching for you for this, and she died content knowing that she gave her life for that of your son, your son together," I said, emphasizing the word 'together'. Henri still did not move, and I could not see if he was struck still by the joy, or the grief, or the shock, or the uncertainty…

Suddenly he looked up, his eyes brilliant not from tears, but from pure joy.

"It means that Francoise is still alive, not just in your heart and mine, but truly here in her son….in my son.." he said slowly. "What is he called?"

"Henri." I said smiling, my shoulders lifting slightly.

Henri smiled broadly. "Heinrich Schulz II, called little Henri…." he said, rubbing his open collar.

"I will take you to see him. He is at home……he has Francoise's eyes," I said, looking up at him. Henri smiled again, and began walking.

I began to walk beside him, arms swinging by my sides, every so often grazing the arm of Henri.

"You have not changed so much since the last time that I have seen you," I said.

"You have though…..You are much taller, and your hair is longer. And you have become much prettier. You will be a particular beauty, I think. A wild beauty," he responded.

"I seem wild because of my dress," I laughed softly. "I am not exactly dressed with elegance," but I could see that Henri was still suffering greatly from the loss of Francoise, even through his joy at the thought of having a son.

"How old are you now?" he asked.

"Fifteen…sixteen in March…"

"You are practically grown already…how time passes!" he sighed.

"What will you do now?" I asked.

"I think that I shall stay here with the old couple…."

"But how? What will you do about your

officer?" I interrupted. "They must know that we are not there by now....what will he do?"

"Nothing – he will not have the chance," he replied simply.

"You cannot wish to kill him! You cannot have truly taken those stupid ideas of the Nazis seriously! I believed that you only enlisted to have a way to return to France!"

"In fact, little one, that is the truth. I do not have the slightest intention of killing him, even if he deserves it as much as every other Nazi snake." Henri's look was cold and his mouth tight.

"And so, what will you do?" I asked curiously.

"I will knock him out, pack him on his horse and send him off. He will never remember the road to this house. It was truly only luck that brought us to you, and you and I together," he said.

"Maybe it was fate," I replied, watching him.

"Maybe," he said, bending his face to the ground again, his hands clasped behind his back.

And we began to walk again, neither of us speaking until we arrived back at the little stone house.

"Shhh.." he placed his fingers across his lips, signaling me to stay quiet. We lay in wait behind a great tree where no one could see us, watching the house where the uniformed officer stood talking agitatedly to the old couple, waving his hands in the air and shouting in German now and again.

"He is saying that if they do not tell where we are, he will kill them," whispered Henri.

I gasped, fearing for them, and seeing a large branch on the ground near my feet, reacted only from instinct. Without warning, I felt my body crouch, my arm stretching out to grasp the branch. Henri watched, dumfounded. Then with a jump I rose, straightening my legs and launching myself against the back of the unsuspecting soldier. I remember only seeing my arm bring the branch down with all of my force against his unprotected head. I remember hearing Marlen cry out, the thud of the soldier as his body hit the earth, Henri running towards us, and suddenly seeing my hand, my hand that had just beat the man lying before me coming back towards me.....or my face......and then everything turned black.

"She is opening her eyes!" I heard a voice in the darkness. Was it a mistake, or had I heard the voice before? Then something moved, and a ray of light appeared in the darkness. The light vanished.

"She has closed them again…"

Of what was that voice so familiar to me speaking? Who was opening and closing her eyes? Looking around, I saw only darkness, and I realized that they were talking about me, and so I forced myself to open my eyes. They were filled suddenly with the morning light, and as it cleared there appeared the plump face of Marlen. She was smiling, as usual, and she laid a cool cloth on my forehead.

"She seems to be awake," she said, turning to Alfredo and Henri, towering over the body of the soldier.

"Did I kill him?" I asked fearfully.

"No – you gave him a great lump, but it probably would not have been too difficult if you had wanted to!" Alfredo said, watching me and laughing.

"Do not listen to that old man, dear – it is only a bruise. In a few days it will be gone," his wife reassured me.

"Yes, but it will leave him dazed enough that he will never remember where he was or how it happened," Alfredo was still laughing, but it was apparent that he still remembered his medical training well.

I tried to arise, putting my hands behind me for support, but immediately I was overcome with a pain in my head, and I lay down holding my head in my hands. Henri was useless at the moment. He was in front of Henri, the little one, watching him intently as he sat in the crib that Alfredo had made for him. I raised myself up again, even though it made my head pound anew.

"But you were quite silly to hit yourself in the head also!" Alfred was enjoying himself.

"Who is this man?" Marlen asked me quietly, helping me to get to my feet.

"He is Henri's father," I answered, passing by the old woman and going to Henri. The young man stood still, watching the little one. Weeping gently, but with a great smile upon his face, he turned to me:

"He is truly my son!" his voice, filled with pride, was filled with wonder also.

"Look – he has the mouth just like mine! And that tiny mole! That mole that I have also! Look! He even has the little finger crooked as mine is!" he exclaimed, overcome with joy, leaning over the crib.

There he was. The little one smiled, looking with wide eyes at his father. Alfredo and Marlen came closer also, watching with compassion this man who took now the babe in his arms. We all watched Henri, seeing easily the depth of the love that this man felt already for the son that he had only just met. Turning to us with shining eyes, holding the tiny, plump hand of the baby, he said:

"Do you realize that this is my son? MY

son!" he spoke almost as if trying to convince himself still that he had helped to conceive such a creature. I smiled, holding still the cloth to my pounding head. I understood that this was a special moment, indescribably sweet and precious, and I wished for it never to end.

Some months passed after that morning in August, and things seemed to brighten up. Henri was growing extraordinarily quickly, and we could see by his proportions that he would probably be quite tall in a few years. Alfredo and Marlen had become like family to us, and we to them, grandparents and grandchildren all in the same house.

The days passed so quickly, from the baby's first laugh, to the first rain of autumn, to the birthday of Francoise. That day we all stayed quiet, remembering and missing the young girl that we had loved. But like so many other things, even that day passed soon, and we found ourselves in December, only a few days before

Christmas.

It was snowing, and we were all beginning to feel the spirit of this holiday. We had decorated the house, and on the hearth there burned always now a great fire. I adored the warmth of the air that I breathed there, after I had been outside in the snow and cold. Even Henri had become somewhat lighthearted, pulling us all from the sadness into which we had fallen after the death of my Francoise.   It had helped immensely also the presence of 'Petit Henri', the name that we gave him to keep from confusing father and son. Everything seemed to be going wonderfully, and we had even organized a proper Christmas dinner, to be held on the *Vigilia*, Christmas Eve.

It happened that on just that night that I fell in love, I think. It all started that evening, when, gathered around the golden wood table that Alfredo had made that year, we heard another knock on the door. Outside, it was snowing, and even stranger, it was the eve of Christmas, the *Vigilia*, so it was quite strange to find someone out and about, especially in the countryside.

I rose to open the door for our mysterious visitor. I pulled open the door, feeling a strong blast of cold air blow into the warm house. The figure in front of me was covered in tattered shirt and jacket, scarf and cap – so covered that I could not make out even if it was male or female, nor have any idea of the age of our visitor. I beckoned for the figure to enter, and closing the door, I wondered if I had done well to let it in. Who could this be that traveled alone, dressed in rags, on the *Vigilia*? In the meantime, the creature began to unwind the scarves and remove the hat that had kept out almost none of the cold, and slowly I began to distinguish its figure. It was a young man, I could tell finally.

First came the hair: a great mass of dark curls that fell almost to the shoulders; then coal black eyes and full soft mouth that hid teeth just a bit irregular; and finally the body of the creature, agile and muscular. His skin was almost amber, and despite looking a bit ill, probably from his long journey, he was a beautiful young man. I felt drawn to him instantly. When he had finished unwrapping all of the layers that he had worn about him, he smiled, and his long sharp teeth, gleaming in the lamplight, gave him an almost wild appearance. But his eyes, framed with long dark lashes, were gentle and sweet.

"Thank you for saving me," he said, looking first at me, and then at the rest of our little group seated around the table. "If it were not for you, I would still be out there waiting to freeze!" he smiled genuinely. It was obvious that he was exhausted and that the food on the table was an overwhelming attraction, but his cordial manner and his character, social and polite, held him back.

"I am called Leo Mavitz," he said, extending a hand that was large and cold. From his name I recognized that he was Hebrew, but it was not upsetting to me at all.

He must have been truly tired and hungry, yet without thinking twice, he had given his Hebrew name, even considering that we found ourselves in these times of terrible intolerance for his race, and he knew nothing of us or the sort of people we might be. He continued to extend his hand to each person at the table, watching the expressions of each one as he pronounced his name each time. When he had finished, he looked perplexed, as though trying to gauge whether we were or were not favourable to the Nazism in the country. After a moment, Henri understood, and he stood. Putting an arm around the young man's shoulders, he said smiling,

"Have no fear here – we are not Nazis inside this house. Would you like something to eat? You seem famished, and we have an abundance of good food to share!"

"Of course, please sit down; here is a place for you," continued Marlen, happily indicating an empty chair.

"Marlen has made a feast, Leo. Help yourself!" smiled Alfredo.

Only I did not speak, but I could not tear my eyes from this young man who, in that moment of desperate hunger and need, ate gracefully and with restraint, hiding his desperation behind his education and upbringing. Seating myself, I was aware of Leo's gaze upon my face, and blushing, I turned, pretending it was nothing. I began to eat while the others threw a storm of questions at the newcomer.

"Where do you come from dear?" asked Marlen, from the opposite side of the table.

"From Paris. I have been hiding for a long time, since just a short while after the war started. I lost my way, and there were weeks that I would hide in the countryside to escape the Nazis."

"And your parents?" asked Henri, who lately had become devoted to his family, made up of our little group.

"They were killed by Nazis," he said, his voice low, shaking his head softly.

"I am sorry…I did not think…" Henri hurried to apologize.

"Do not worry, I am sure that I am not the only one who has suffered in this war," he said with such wistfulness. "You seem, however, a family above all happy with each other!" he said smiling, suddenly rousing from his melancholy.

"Oh, we are not a family of blood, but a family of affection," Marlen told him sweetly.

"Ah, so you two are not their children?" he asked Henri and me.

"No…in fact, our story is a tragedy like

yours," said the young German, hiding under his smile an expression of still-fresh pain.

"Ah, then you two are married?" Leo continued, looking in my direction.

"No no! He is the love of my sister!" I exclaimed, suddenly frantic to push from his mind the idea that I might be already with someone.

"Then who is the man lucky enough to be with such a lovely girl?" he asked me gently.

"There is no one. He has not found me yet......I think," I said, half smiling at him.

"Ahh...you never know: fate never ceases to play with our lives!" he said seriously, looking me directly in the eyes.

Marlen came into the modest room just then from the kitchen, carrying with her another great plate of food, and the conversation between Leo and me was interrupted. We passed the evening like that, talking, listening, and the presence of Leo was delightful to us all, as he told wonderful fantastic stories. My favorite was one his grandmother had told him, referring to his cousin Moshe, who had never taken a wife or had children.

"Moshe – get up!" called Leo's Aunt Ruth to her son Moshe.

"But I don't want to return to school!" he complained.

"Get up this moment," his mother cried.

"I do not want to go – the children tease me and kick me, and the professors do not like me! Give me a good reason to go!" proposed Moshe.

"Moshe, you are forty years old and the headmaster!" his mother said in exasperation.

And Leo went on, making us all laugh with his funny voices and impressions, and his silly expressions. I had a wonderful time that evening, I remember. And I remember how deeply he had struck me, this young man with his gentle ways and his soft expressions. Before I slept that night, I could not stop thinking of him, and under my breath I practiced 'Madame Mavitz' as I had done when I was a child enamoured of some boy.

"Good morning!" came a deep voice from behind me. I turned. Behind me stood Leo, leaning against the doorjamb, grinning.

"Happy Christmas!" I said happily, smiling at him. I turned around completely, still lying in my bed, cozy under the covers.

"For you this is a different *festa*, is it not?" I asked curiously.

"Yes. It is the celebration of Hannukah. The celebration lasts for eight days, and represents the consecration of the temple in Jerusalem. I did not think you knew about it," he told me.

"Good Hannukah then," I smiled again, and sat up a bit in the bed.

I watched him. Taking away all of those scraps that covered him when he arrived, he was left with a simple grey shirt, a pair of dark pants that were worn and frayed, a pair of leather suspenders and a pair of black shoes. He must have been well-to-do before the war broke out, judging from the clothes he wore, even though they were ruined from the journey he had made. The evening before I saw on his coat the Star of David sewn on the sleeve. It was incredible to think of what was happening, but for the most part I was no longer in contact with the news of the war, and so I had no real understanding of how truly grave the situation had become for the Hebrews. It seemed odd, but Leo did not seem so devastated by the war, and kept up an attitude more or less lighthearted for us all.

I turned to the window. Outside, the snow glistened in the brilliant sunshine. Suddenly I wanted desperately to go out there.

"Can we go outside?" I turned again to

Leo.

"Outside? But it is incredibly cold today!" he exclaimed, coming closer.

"But please! A short walk will only do you good!" I tried to convince him.

"Oh, alright! Get dressed then. I will go to get my scarf and coat," he said, smiling as he left, closing the door of my room behind him. I rose quickly and chose a dress of blue and white that Marlen had made for me. It was nothing special as dresses go, but everyone said that it flattered me, and the color went well with my fair complexion. I donned the long dress quickly, brushed my hair and threw on my heavy blue woolen jacket. As I came out of my room, I realized that I had forgotten my shoes, and I ran back to get them.

Finally I arrived in the kitchen, where Leo was waiting for me patiently. This time he had put on only a jacket and scarf to keep himself warm. Opening the door with one arm, he turned awkwardly, indicating that I should go ahead of him.

"Ladies first," he said with grace. I smiled

and passed with my head high, thanking him with grace of my own. Outside, I felt a cold shiver run up my spine, but I did not want to lose the chance to be alone with him for a bit, and so, taking a deep breath, I turned to him and said enthusiastically:

"Courage! Let's go!"

Leo grinned at me, and unexpectedly took my hand in his, with a confidence and ease that seemed as if we had known each other for years. For the rest, I truly felt that way. Walking hand in hand for a while, talking of this and of that. Without warning he stopped in a sort of natural clearing, circled about with trees, and bending down, he formed between his two hands a snowball. Rising, he threw it right at me suddenly, laughing. I stopped still for a moment, covered in snow and shocked, but in only a moment the surprise passed, and I crouched in the snow to make my own snowballs. Jumping up, I aimed for him and threw.

"Now the war begins!" I cried happily, dodging a hit.

We played wildly for ten minutes or so,

until I fell to the ground exhausted, ignoring the fact that we would be wetter than ever from laying in the snow.

"How old are you?" Leo asked me, stretched out close by.

"I will be sixteen in March. You?" I answered, turning to look at him.

"Seventeen. I was seventeen on the 13th of October."

"Ten days before Francoise."

"Who is Francoise?" he asked, sitting up slightly and supporting his head on his elbows.

"My sister," I said, still fallen in the snow.

"The wife of Henri?"

"They were never able to be married," I told him, remembering.

"But she was the mother of 'Petit Henri", yes?"

"Yes…"

"But now where is she?"

"She died…" I answered, my voice as cold as the snow.

"Forgive me – I did not intend to anger you," Leo apologized.

"No, no…it is me who reacts badly still to her death. It is only that my life seems to become harder and harder."

"Tell me," he said gently.

"Tell you?" I repeated, looking up into his face.

"*Si*, tell me…" he prodded again ever so gently.

"No, first tell me what has happened to you. Then I will tell you everything."

"Very well," he sighed deeply, moving again close to me, his cold hand grazing mine. "It all started when I was about twelve. Until that day we were a perfectly normal family, not badly situated, typical in Paris. We were mother, father and three children, of whom I was the youngest."

"What were they called?" I interrupted.

"My sister was Rachel, and my brother Ari. Ari was older, twenty when he was first captured by the Germans. Rachel instead was eighteen. We had always gone along together, we three, even though Ari had always been the most aggressive and the most protective of the family, and of me and my sister. I had a good relation with my parents also, who supported me in my decision to become a painter. Then, however, the war broke out, and the Hebrews were the targets, something of a change." Leo laughed sadly.

"The day that the Germans invaded Paris, I was out of the city, and so they did not take me. I remember that, reentering the city on a little used street on which the Germans had not yet posted guards, I knew immediately that something terrible had happened. Returning to my home, I passed behind bushes and trees and other houses, being careful not to let the soldiers see me. They were everywhere, marching through the streets, passing in groups of four or five to check the quarter for any Hebrew that they had missed. When I arrived at the main street of the quarter, I saw a long line of people under the order of armed soldiers, and in the midst there were many people that I knew. There were the Horowitz', and the Suvitz family, old Madame Agnes and so on. They were all Hebrews anyway; you could see from the Stars sewn on their coats.

"Among them there was also my family,

all of them being divided according to gender. In moments there were two lines where before there was one, women to the right, men to the left……..I remember the fear on Rachel's face as she held tight to the hand of my mother, and the fury that burned in Ari's eyes. Ari had always been stubborn, and a little violent, and the fact that he now found himself in this dangerous situation did not diminish that ire. In fact, he could not restrain himself when the German soldiers began playing jokes on the men, showering blows on the oldest of them. When one dealt my father a blow on the head, Ari flung himself with all of his might against the soldier, screaming. I remember the pain that I felt deep inside of me when, from the relative safety of the edifice behind which I hid, I watched the soldier pull out his pistol and shoot straight at Ari, over and over again. He was hit in the stomach and the chest, and he died.

"My mother screamed and burst into tears, and my father bowed his head before the body of his son, lifting his eyes to the soldier and laying a curse upon his head. And that soldier, still infuriated by the blows he dealt my brother, needed no encouragement to kill my father also, one bullet straight to his head. My father fell to the ground dead, his body falling over that of my brother.

"By this time the others were almost all herded upon two great wagons, including my mother and sister, crying and screaming hysterically. The soldiers jumped into a car and departed, followed by the wagons filled with Hebrews destined for the concentration camps. The bodies of my father and brother, instead stayed there in the street, one over the other, their blood mixing together to stain the street below them. I could not get near them, even as they lay there, and I began to run.

"I ran and ran, not stopping until I could not stand any longer upon my legs, and my lungs were bursting for oxygen. I found myself in the outermost zone of the city, where it began to give way to the countryside, and small villages replaced the bustle of the main city. I turned toward the countryside, and began to run again. I did not know where I was going, nor did I have food or water, but I knew that I would never turn back. I ran, using all of my force, until the night came, and exhausted, I threw myself against an oak tree, kicking and fighting, until I could move no longer, and then I wept. I wept through the night, dreaming and awake.

"I found myself then more or less in the countryside, and I stayed there until I was forced to move to find food. From that day to this, I have walked, hiding from the Germans, moving constantly, determined to stop only when I was forced to by need.

"I have never found a place like this, though. It is completely lost to the world."

"Will you stay here then?" I asked hopefully.

"Yes, probably. It depends much on the will of the DeNeri's, if they want me to stay or not."

"Of course they will want you to stay! They are the most good-hearted people in this world. They have given solace and affection not just to me but to Henri also when he was in need, and surely they will give it to you also," I assured him.

"Well, we will see," he replied, and his voice found the lighthearted note that it had lost during his storytelling. "But now, it is your turn….go ahead, tell me your story!" And Leo turned again to me, as if to put his full concentration into what I was about to tell him.

"Well, before everything, I must tell you that my father died when I was very young, and my sister Francoise and I lived only with my mother until the beginning of '38. It was then that my mother disappeared, so unexpectedly, and we have never seen her again. Francoise and I lived alone for nearly a year in our house in Paris. It was a terribly lonely time for us. Then, in the summer of 1939, Francoise met Henri and fell in love with him, and she came with child soon after. Unfortunately, she did not discover this until Henri had departed, returning to Germany to care for his mother, just at the beginning of the war. They were so in love, those two, and he had promised to return for her quickly, but one day she received a letter from Germany, saying that before he could return for her, he felt compelled to go to Berlin to help the resistance, to try to stop the insanity of Hitler. Francoise became mad with fear, sure that he would be killed, and refused to stay in Paris. She was determined to go to Germany to find him and stop him, even though she knew that it would be nearly impossible. Obviously I could not abandon her, eighteen years old and carrying a child, to start off on her own in the midst of a war, and so we left Paris together. We walked, day after day, Francoise becoming more and more fragile, more and more sickly. One night on the roadside, even though it was too soon by at least several weeks, Francoise brought her child into the light, but the effort was too much for her in her weakened state, and she died there as the babe was born. I was alone with the little one, lost in the countryside….I had no idea even where we were. I had to bury my sister, my Francoise…….I promise you that I had never imagined such a disastrous feeling as that….After that there were days of desperation before I could bring myself to leave there, and I took the babe, who I called Henri, to honor his father and the love that Francoise had for him, and finally came to this house, with Mssr. DeNeri. They received me with arms open, and offered me shelter here with them, because Paris had fallen to the Germans, and they wanted company here. We passed months like this. Then, in the summer of this year past, 1940, there came to the house two Nazi soldiers. One of them was Henri. He had joined the hated Nazis for love of Francoise, to return as quickly as possible to Paris to find her. I promise you he has no Nazi sympathy, have no fear!

"Anyway, that night I took him to see the grave of Francoise, and I told him of little Henri. He decided also to stay here, and after that you know the rest....I am sorry if I tell less than every small detail, but I still do not think happily of what has happened in these past months.....I do not like the memories......."

Leo watched me for a moment, then smiled gently and said,

"Come, let us leave here before we are completely drenched from the snow," and standing, he brushed the flakes from his shoulders and pants, and extended his warm hand to me, helping me up. We began to walk towards the house.

"We have both passed through great sadness to come here, but perhaps our destiny holds something grand and wonderful yet," I said hopefully, looking up at him.

"Perhaps it was destiny that brought us two together," he replied, tucking my hand into his again. I did not speak, but I held tightly to his hand then. We returned to the house, wet with snow and frozen, but happy that morning….happy that day, for between me and Leo there had come an accord more perfect than any I had ever felt with another. I loved him more every day after that, but I was not sure if he felt the same for me. I knew though, that he was also happy to spend time with me – we had the same tastes, the same likes and dislikes, the same ideas of life. There were many times that we thought the same thoughts at the same time, or made the same gestures, or even said the same words together. I had never felt so complete with anyone, and his presence gave me courage for the future.

I remember the day that we first kissed. It was not my first – when I was younger, in school, I had kissed on the mouth a boy from my class, and later he kissed me again in the park, but for such a long time I had not allowed myself to think of love, not for me. Leo and I were sitting on the floor in front of the fire one evening, drying and warming ourselves after another walk in the snow. We were just talking, of nothing in particular, when suddenly he looked at me intently.

"You are beautiful," he said.

"No, it's not true," I answered, looking down in surprise.

"No, it is true. I think that I must be in love with you," he said, with an ironic twist in his voice.

"Please don't tease me Leo," I boxed him once on the shoulder.

"No, I am not joking. You are fantastic! How could I not be in love with you?" He seemed so content at the thought.

"Leo, I…but…." I stammered pathetically.

"Ah….you are not happy about this. I am sorry – I did not intend to make you uncomfortable," he said quickly, sincerely.

"No, Leo, it is not that! I also…I ….that is….."

Leo grinned, and taking my face in his hand, he leaned near and kissed me. Such a long, sweet kiss…… When it was over, he smiled again at me, and rising, went to his room. I remained there, by the fire, my heart beating crazily, my hands trembling, but filled with such a feeling of happiness that I had never known. I asked myself how it was possible that I, an orphan at sixteen, and Leo, a French Hebrew, could be so similar and so attracted to each other, but it was better not wondering, and I thought then only of the wonderful things that were happening in my life just then. For the moment my life was perfect, but the feeling that this would not last, that these happy moments were fleeting, and that life would cease soon to be so simple and perfect, began to rise in me. I tried not to listen to these feelings, not to notice that all around us news of the world and of the war grew worse and worse, but it was not possible for long.

Oh yes….it was not for much longer that we were able to live so simply, so peacefully. We were so afraid that soon even here would come the Nazis, and we began to speak of precautions against that in the house and among ourselves. Often I heard Leo and Henri talking together, voices low, but especially after Henri went to town to buy supplies for us, as he did the third Friday of every month.

"I have seen them again today. They walk about town freely, and everyone fears them. I am afraid that they will find even our small place here in the next few weeks. They are closer every day. They are not so hostile to the French, these Germans that have been posted here, but they will not tolerate the presence of Jews. I am afraid that if they come here, even though they will probably not harm the rest of us, if they find you they will kill you, or worse, send you away to one of the concentration camps the way that they have all of the others. I believe that we must find someplace safe for you, where you can reach quickly and remain hidden away, in case they arrive unexpectedly here one day." I heard Henri, his French nearly perfect, but still the trace of German in his accent.

Leo only nodded his head in agreement, but his eyes were dark and thoughtful, and it was clear that his thoughts were far away.

I remember a discussion that we had one of the last times that we walked in the countryside, walking like we had all winter. Following that same familiar road that we took so often, Leo took my hand, and we walked side by side, enclosed in the spring that was blossoming everywhere. Neither of us had spoken, on all of that long walk, but I knew that he had to tell me something, and I felt a wave of confusion and sadness without even knowing what the words would be. I saw the tiny green leaves, budding from branches that only a short time ago were covered in an icy glaze; birds, returned from their migration, singing happily, seeming to dance on their perches in time with the leaves that moved gently in the breeze that passed, still crisp from the winter; but everything seemed wrong, as though we were better to find ourselves still in winter, the skeletons of trees etched across the grey seasonal sky, and all signs of life, both human and animal, hidden, waiting for the spring. But inside of me I felt no change, and I looked about me at the spring and the freshness of the season, and resigned myself to accept whatever he said to me in that inappropriate place, all the while praying secretly that it would perhaps be something unimportant, nothing to worry for.

Leo had often mentioned bits of an idea of his to leave here sooner or later, knowing that he could not hide forever, and wanting to escape before the Germans arrived in this hidden place. With everywhere nearby already under the dominion of the Nazis, he knew that he could not remain unobserved much longer. Fearing what he would have to say, but knowing that he had made whatever decision that he must, I knew that whatever he had decided, it would be even more for our benefit than for his, and that I could not put my feelings before the logic of what he had determined to do. I knew Leo by this time almost five months, and I loved him already terribly, but I knew also what he would have to endure if he stayed here with us, hidden and fearing for his life.

We arrived in the glade where we had stopped to talk on our first walk together, that Christmas morning that seemed to have passed years and years ago. Leo sat upon a rock warmed by the sun, and I sat beside him, my hand still tightly held in his larger, warmer one. He looked at me with eyes narrowed against the first rays of the spring sun, that shone directly in his face, and I felt his hand pull mine closer, tighter. I looked into his face, surrounded by the dark hair that shone and curled slightly, like the light branches that curled and knotted in the tree nearby, the same tree where I climbed often during our visits to this place that we now considered ours. Leo opened his mouth, as if to speak, but closed it again, having no words, I think.

"Leo, tell me what you must and let us finish this," I pleaded, nervous and fearful.

"It is difficult for me to tell you this…you

know that I love you, and that I have no wish to leave you, but it has become necessary for me to depart. I have stayed here nearly half of the year, and have lived in a peace and serenity that I had not known for ages before, but part of me has always known that it would be finished, sooner or later. The Germans, the Nazis, are always closer, and each day we hear tales of their conduct, always more violent and more aggressive. I am afraid that I must leave you. This is no longer the place for me, but it is still your home, and you must not let your life be ruined for a poor Hebrew like me.........I am leaving within the week, as soon as I am able to prepare supplies and find a way to arrive safely at the coast. From there, I will board a ship and go to America, as many Hebrews before me have done. There I will be free to profess my religion and to live in peace.

"You must know, however, that I do not do all of this happily. It will be terrible for me to leave.......to leave my country, my friends here..........you............" He was solemn, watching me with eyes that had darkened like the night, but brilliant as the stars that live there.

I could not speak. Every atom, every particle of me, seemed disattached from every other, moving in an emptiness that was dark and frightening. I did not want to leave Leo. I could not do it. Never…..Never.

"I love you too much," I whispered, pulling my hand from under his. Jumping up, I ran from him, from the horrible thoughts that overflowed in my mind. Somehow I hoped that escaping from him I could also escape from the sadness, but even as I ran, I knew that no matter how far or how fast, I could not hide from my heart that which my mind knew already.

Leo was leaving.

Forever.

To America.

Far away.

Too far…………

Throwing myself against the black trunk of the nearest tree, my legs too tired to hold me, I slid to the ground, crying and desolate.

Returning home later, worn and exhausted, I found Leo sitting on the stoop of the house. His golden face was locked in an expression of deep, distant thought, his head supported by a fist clenched tightly, his eyes fixed, unseeing, on a point in the small garden that we kept near the house. As I neared, Leo became aware of my presence, and rising, he brushed the dust of the step from his pants. I stopped, and he came to meet me.

"I cannot let you leave. I will die if I must watch you leave. I have already seen what can happen when two who love each other so are separated. I do not want to end that way," I told him, thinking sadly of Francoise.

"You did not let me finish talking, little one. I wanted to tell you that I am forced to leave, but you have the freedom still to move about as you please, to stay here or to go. I wanted to ask you to come with me, but you ran away. I nearly followed you, but you needed time to think, so I waited. If I must leave without you, I do not know if I will live to see the coast, my pain will be so great." As he spoke, he took my hand in his and looked me directly in the eyes. "In any case, the decision is yours. I cannot be sure to convince you to come to America with me, but I want only to say that I have never loved as I have loved in these last months. I feel complete only with you. We are twin spirits, and I hope only that you feel the same," he said, and I felt his uncertainty and his insecurity, which till now, I had thought that only I felt. I knew then that also for me, he was a part of my life, of my spirit, that I could neither leave nor lose. Without warning overcome with emotion, I wrapped my arms around his collar and laid my head on his shoulder. He held me tight to him, and I could feel the silent tears that shook him. In my mind for an instant I saw Elodie, her pale arms tight around my neck. I detached myself from Leo, and looking in his eyes, I felt overpowered by such a wave of tenderness and sadness and love. Seeing his cheeks, streaked with transparent tears, I whispered,

"I will go with you. I will never leave you," and coming closer again to him I kissed him, my cheeks too wet with the salty tears that coursed down from my tightly closed eyes.

That evening, Leo and I were to tell Marlen, Alfredo and Henri our decision to leave together for America. It would not be easy for either Leo or me, and particularly for the old DeNeri's, who had become so affectionate with us. We had become their adopted family. As close as if we were truly their children. And with Henri, we had a bond like brothers and sisters; he adored passing time talking with Leo, and they had become fast friends. I did not know how we would be able to leave this house and its inhabitants, but I intended to concentrate on the future, and the possibilities that might present themselves on our arrival. I began to think about writing again, perhaps publishing in that new world some story that I might put on paper, or some small poems. Leo was hopeful also, and had determined to take on again his dream of painting once we arrived and settled, with work and home found and in place.

In the meantime, though, we were still in France, in the midst of the extermination of the Hebrews, and we needed desperately to move ourselves quickly to arrive at the coast as soon as possible.

That evening, time seemed to stand still, and each of us lived every second as though it were a year. And of those years, each was different from the others: we laughed, and joked and told stories, looking forward to the departure as a great adventure in one; in the next we talked quietly, discussing and explaining the various ways in which our lives had intertwined; still later we wept and we remembered....remembered the days that we had passed together. And so, year after year, second after second the evening passed, making space for us in that dark, sad night, until finally we reached the end of our conversations and our dinner, and each of us returned reluctantly to bed, none of us able all the same to sleep.

"My dear, I want to show you something," Mssr. DeNeri called to me the day before we were to depart.

I followed him into the bedroom of the old couple, where a small lamp illuminated the top of the dark wood bureau, giving a festive air to the modest room. I stopped at the entrance of the room, not sure to follow him completely in, but Alfredo had turned to a chest that sat under the window. The old man kneeled in front of it with difficulty, lifting the top open with gnarled, marked hands. He had aged much in the past year, and old to begin with, he tired now easily. I was glad that now there was Henri here to help him, so he would not have to tire himself so much each day.

From the open chest came the soft sweet odor of old paper, like the old books in the library that I visited with Mama', when she was still alive. Inside there were pieces of carefully torn newspaper on which could be read titles: "Boy Killed in Auto Accident! Parents Heartbroken", "Young Man Run Down", and "Killed on the Streets of Paris". There was also an old soldier's uniform, maps and medical books, an old, faded photo and a pair of baby shoes. Alfredo beckoned me to come and sit near him. Kneeling beside him, I watched him finger the baby shoes affectionately.

"They were Tommy's," he said smiling. "We bought them in a shop on the Champs Elysee', and when we put them on him, he pulled them off right away. He was barely a year old, and hated to wear any shoes on his feet. Eventually, he put them on his hands, and refused to take them off. It was enough to come near him and try to touch them, to free his hands and put them on his feet, for him to begin to scream and protest. He was a mischievous, bright boy!" The old man's expression was sorrowful and sweet.

"This was him, my Tommy," he said, taking the photograph from the chest and handing it to me to see. In the photo, a beautiful girl with violet blue eyes smiled happily, her shoulders wrapped in the arm of a young man who appeared to be of my age. He had dark hair and eyes, and I knew they were green, like those of Alfredo, from the description that Marlen had given once of him. His smile was that of an angel and that of a devil all at once, and he had a deep dimple on his right cheek. Across his fine nose, like that of his mother Marlen, clearly the woman in the photograph so happily beside him, were sprinkled many small freckles, spreading from eye to eye, and finally losing themselves in the blush of his cheeks, obvious even in the grey tones of the old photo.

He would have been tall as Alfredo, for he was already a few centimetres taller than Marlen in the picture. He was slender, but his arms and shoulders were well shaped and muscular, and his eyes shone with a clear and true happiness. It seemed as though a light radiated from within that young man, and from the woman he held so affectionately. I imagined miserably the pain and desperation that the old couple must have felt at the death of that beautiful boy, who was so clearly happy in life with them. While I looked at the photograph, Alfredo had pulled out the newspapers and was reading them again, his eyes bright and wet. When he saw me watching, he put down the papers immediately and smiled bravely, trying to escape the sadness…

"Look – this was my uniform when I fought with the Italian soldiers. What a grand country, Italia! It is a terrible shame that now there is Mussolini at the head of the government….what a fool…but Italia will come again into its splendor, because it is a strong and proud nation!" his voice filled with pride, and he pulled out the slightly ruined uniform, worn a bit about the seams and knees, but well tended all the same.

It was not difficult to imagine him, young

and tall and beautiful, dressed smartly in the Italian military uniform, at the time of the first great War. But now he was old, and had become my dear friend and protector, and seated here by me on the floor with the old uniform in his hand, the memories sprinkled through his mind like the stars in the night sky, now clearer and more brilliant as he remembered.

After a bit, Alfredo roused himself from his reverie, and looking in the chest again, lifted out his old medical books. They were dusty and unused for ages, but they still had intact the red covers ornately decorated with threads of gold. He set aside the uniform on the floor near him, and lifted up higher on his knees, to see better the inside of the chest, searching under the maps and papers that remained. Grasping at something that remained hidden in the bottom of the chest, he smiled widely, watching me. He lifted his arm from the chest, carrying in his hand an old metal box, covered in rust. I watched curiously as Alfredo placed it carefully on the floor and put his arm back into the chest again. I saw him push aside some of the papers lining the bottom of the old chest, and draw out a small linen sack. On the widest side of the sack were embroidered finely the initials 'T.D.N.'

Tommaso DeNeri, I thought immediately. I watched while Alfredo opened the embroidered sack and turned it upside down over his outstretched hand. From the sack slid a tiny key, pounded from the same metal as the rusty box sitting there on the floor. The old man picked up the key, and holding it gingerly between his thumb and index finger, he guided it gently into the latch on the box that he had taken from the chest. Turning it carefully, the cover of the box moved slightly, and from the opening came the faint odor of dust and age.

Alfredo slowly opened the metal box, fingers trembling. Inside lay a necklace from which was hung a strange charm. Looking at it more closely, I saw that the charm was actually a bullet, drilled with a hole in the middle of it, to allow the necklace to pass through. Next to it lay an envelope, yellowed with age. Alfredo lifted the necklace and passed it gently through his thin fingers.

"This bullet saved my life," he said, his eyes wide and bright. "I remember everything as though it were yesterday: the war, the enemy….the dead…..This bullet, my dear, hit me in the arm, and I lost a great deal of blood quickly. I fell from the pain and the blood loss, and hit my head against a rock, losing consciousness. The enemy, seeing me as they passed by lying on the ground in a pool of blood, believed that I was already dead, and so did not waste another shot on me, as they did on many of my companions and friends. Thanks to this, I lived, and was sent home to recover to Marlen and Tommaso."

He smiled at the memory, moving closer to the window to inspect the bullet.

"Every time I wear this around my neck, my fortune increases, and the misfortunes disappear. I lost it before Tommy was killed, and had not seen it for years. But even more strange…..some months before you arrived, I found it again, sitting on a table. Marlen says that she did not find it, and I did not either see it before that. It is my amulet. My good luck piece.

I fear that if I lose it again, some new and terrible misfortune will befall us, as happened when we lost our Tommy. And so instead, I give it to you, to carry with you good fortune and health. But keep it close, my little one: if you lose it, it will be the end." He placed the chain around my neck.

"But if I take it you will have misfortune. I cannot!" I cried, feeling the weight of the 'charm' hanging around my neck.

"No, dearest. I know inside that this small treasure has done enough for me - saving my life, returning me to Tommy and Marlen, and now sending to me you and Henri and Leo and the little one, all of you like a new family for me. I am certain that giving it to you now will not diminish my good fortune, but will increase yours. In that small bullet that you must keep safe is my love for you. Always remember that," he said to me, smiling with his heart and with his spirit.

Having no words to thank him, I threw my arms about him and hugged him tightly to me, feeling his long arms wrapped around me with affection. It was a moment of tenderness that I would not forget – that great man giving to me his most precious treasure, and telling me that my arrival in his life, lost and desperate as I was, was a great fortune for him. I knew that I loved them both deeply, and that they loved me, but I said nothing that day, for in that moment, those gestures contained more than words ever could.

That evening, at dinner, Alfredo and Marlen announced that they wanted to give us something. Neither of us had any idea of what they were speaking, but when Marlen returned to the kitchen holding an envelope of yellowed paper, I recognized it immediately. It was the envelope from the metal box that Alfredo had opened that morning, giving me the necklace and the good luck piece dangling from it. She sat at the table in her regular place and held out her hand to her husband, the affection that she held for him evident in her violet blue eyes.

"Our dearest young friends, you cannot know how sorrowful we are that you must leave us, but we know also that by now it is essential for your safety Leo, to go. It is for this that Alfredo and I have decided to give you something that will serve you well when you are in America, but also while you travel from here to that far place. You must know that your presence here is always welcome, and that your place is always open in this house, if you should return someday."

"Of course we will come back someday! As soon as the war is over we will come. You must know that this is our country, and neither of us will ever be able to stay away for long. Perhaps we will not return to live here again, but we will return. We promise you this," I interrupted her, jumping to my feet, as if to give force to the sureness I felt.

"Good, my dear. You will both be always in our thoughts and our prayers, and we will await anxiously your first visit." Marlen smiled, handing the envelope to me. I held out my hand to take it from her with gratitude, but she stopped me before I could open it.

"Wait, dearest. You must open the

envelope together, after you have left. You will always remember us, won't you?" she asked with tears in her eyes.

I only smiled at her and nodded, but it was enough for her to understand that I loved her well, and all of the others; her husband, Henri, and my little nephew.

Alfredo did not speak much that evening. He passed the time watching me and Leo, and when Henri asked him what he was doing, he answered simply, tranquilly, that he was memorizing our faces, in case we did not return again. I sat down next to him and smiled at him:

"Do not worry, I will be back, and until that day, we can meet in our dreams, and every time that you dream of me, know that I am thinking of you, and that I am here. Alive or dead, I will be here."

He smiled back at me then, and held my hand tightly for a moment, then began to clap and laugh, to lighten a bit the worry of the evening, and to make us all happier.

Our last evening together, I thought.

I would be back someday, I was sure, but

even as I continued to repeat this to myself, over and over in my sadness to leave, I could not help but watch more closely my friends, my family, to capture before it was too late their images in my mind forever.

Kicking back the blankets, I felt a light shiver run over me, racing coldly up my spine, not from fright or illness, but because I knew it was over. My peace, my safety, was finished. From that day I would be alone with Leo, without a roof or a single person to care for me. But by now I had made my decision, and I did not regret it: I loved Leo, and he loved me, and I was sure that if I stayed here, I would never see him again.

I rose and walked to the chair where I had laid out my clothes for the journey. I put on a pair of men's pants, lightweight and comfortable for traveling; a shirt that had been my mother's, white and embroidered with flowers at the wrists and on the collar, left over from the days when we were all together and something that I hoped would bring luck to us; a pair of boots and a sweater of grey wool that Marlen had made for me. It was early summer, but I was not certain of when we would arrive in America, or in what sort of situations we might find ourselves during the voyage, and so I knew that a wool sweater would serve me well, even if it was warm now. I had turned up the hem of the pants many times, as they were quite long on me, considering that at one time they were part of Alfredo's wardrobe, but I pulled them higher up on my waist, until they reached to just below my knees.

Once I was dressed, I crawled again onto my bed, kneeling before the pillow and reaching under for the necklace and charm of Alfredo. I looked at it for a moment, holding it carefully in my hands, then opening the clasp and laying it about my collar, I closed it around me and latched the rusted hook closed securely again. I pulled my hair from under the chain, feeling the weight of the charm upon my neck, then sighing, I picked up the brush and began to run it through my hair.

My hair had grown quite long over the years, and now it was also often unbearably hot to wear down around my neck, so often I was forced to pull it up above the nape and hold it with a stick or a kerchief. Today, instead, I left it down, dark and wavy, and it began to make me hot quickly. Knowing that it would be impossible to bear if the day became warmer, I balled it onto the top of my head with a light blue kerchief, tying it behind at my neck. I dropped my brush into the opening of the bag that lay at my feet, the bundle that contained my few dresses, some particular treasures of my own, and the food that Marlen had prepared so carefully for us for our travels.

I closed the bag and looked around carefully, sad but resigned to abandon this room that had sheltered me for the last year. I turned and reached out for the yellow envelope that sat on the night table, the envelope that Marlen had given us the evening before. I lifted my foot and set it on the tabletop, slipping the envelope carefully into the space between my leg and the leather, wedging it down low to keep from losing it.

Sadly, I lifted the bag to my shoulder and passed slowly from the room. In the kitchen I found everyone already seated, the breakfast of hot tea and broth a silent affair this morning. I sat in my usual place, placing the bag beside me and sipping slowly the tea that even in memory seemed to scorch my mouth, though it was probably only tepid that morning.

No one spoke; it seemed that we all concentrated on our meal, trying not to think that soon we would be torn apart again, probably forever. I thought of all of the beautiful memories that I would carry with me of this secret place, where we lived almost completely isolated from the terrible war outside. Without warning, a fresh tear slid down my cheek, brown already from the summer sun, and I looked up, addressing my dearest friends there about me:

"I will miss you all so much, you know. I do not know how to say goodby to you, but in one way or another I must. It is useless to pretend that nothing will happen. I love you all, and I pray that only goodness will follow you until the ends of your lives. Also for me it will be so difficult not to have you with me any longer, but I wish that the last moments that we may pass together be more happy than sad and silent." I stood as I spoke.

"You are right, my dear. I will miss you, but it is better that we think of the fantastic opportunity before you now, and that in the end you are not dying – you are saving your lives. As soon as the war ends, you will be able to return, even if only for a while, if you find yourselves well set in America." Marlen smiled at us both, and hugged me to her. I held her tight, and felt two, three, four tears slide down my cheeks.

"I miss you already, Marlen."

"As do I, dearest," she answered, letting me go.

"And you, my dearest Signor Alfredo, who has been my friend and my protector – you I will miss especially," I said, smiling under the tears that would not stop, and I hugged him tightly also.

"I will always be with you, my dearest. I will be in your mind, and your heart and in the charm you carry around your collar, to help you, and to console you when you are frightened, and to guide you when you have need, and to celebrate when you celebrate, and to cry when you cry. I will be always with you……..I will never forget you…..." he whispered to me in my ear, his eyes glistening. I slid my arms from around his neck, standing on my tallest toes, smiled into his eyes, and answered him:

"And I will be always with you, and we will talk in our dreams."

Henri, standing close to me now, pushed into my hands a book that looked new, titled "Poems". I took the book happily, smiling at him.

"I remembered that you always liked poetry, so I thought that you might like this."
I looked at the book. It was bound beautifully, and the pages were splendidly white. It must have come dearly to him, particularly during these lean times of the war.

"I am not good at goodbyes. I am beginning already to cry," he said honestly. "You know that I do not love you only because you are the sister of my beloved, but for all of the things that you are: because you are stubborn, and shy, and courageous and loyal, and because you are my friend. I love you," he said with such tenderness. I could not resist the need to embrace him, and I threw my arms about him, laying my head upon his shoulder. I filled my lungs with his masculine perfume, and for only a moment, everything seemed right, as though nothing unusual were about to happen, as though my world were still in one piece, whole and safe and happy, but it passed, and I drew my arms away slowly from Henri. I smiled again, and stepped to the handmade crib where petit Henri sat, playing and laughing, tugging at my hand when I offered it to him, his chubby fingers clasped tightly around one of mine. He kicked and rolled and laughed happily. I leaned down to him, placing a kiss on his forehead.

"Remember me, little Henri?" I begged, speaking softly. "When I return you will know already how to walk and talk, I imagine. And then, you can tell everything that you have done in this time to your aunt, and I will tell you of your sweet mother, Francoise." And I felt sadness wash over me again, so that I could barely speak the last words. I moved away from the crib to Leo's side as he began to speak to Henri, Alfredo and Marlen:

"I …I….have known you all for such a short time that I am almost embarrassed to profess to you how I will miss you all. I fear that you will think that I think, that I speak, with little sincerity and seriousness, but I must admit to you that if you had not taken me in that Christmas night, now I would surely be dead. Thanks to you, I am able, at least in part, to forget some of the pain and fear that the war has brought to me. You have been a grand comfort to me, both as friends," and he looked at Henri, "and as parents," and he bowed his head to Alfredo and Marlen, "and as love," and he passed his arm about my waist and I smiled. "I will miss you all so much, and I hope with all of my heart that we will be able to return one day to France….to you…..but until then, I will never forget you. Know this from my heart."

Henri embraced Leo as a brother, giving him at the end a friendly slap on the back, and drew away. Leo stood before Alfredo, who took his hand and kissed his cheeks. At the last there remained Marlen, who was especially fond of this sweet, good boy. She embraced him long and hard, then straightened her back, and tugged fondly at his white shirt, putting it just so. The white of the shirt that he wore made his dark eyes seem brilliant, tears glistening in them, and his hair darker than usual against the fabric as it fell in curls across his broad shoulders.

"Thank you for everything," I whispered again, embracing one last time each of my friends there, then taking up the bag and passing it to Leo.

I opened the door, and we began to walk, Leo and I, waving and blowing kisses from our hands to Henri, Alfredo and Marlen, watching us sadly from the door of the little house.

We had walked hours when we stopped for the first time, tired and hungry. I sat under a tree by the roadside, and took from the bag an old water bottle that Alfredo had used in the war. Swallowing the fresh water, washing off my face and hands, I was careful to use only a bit. I passed the bottle to Leo, who had sat down beside me in the meantime. Looking around, I laid my head against the trunk of the tree behind me, and suddenly I thought of the envelope that the old couple had given us, that we were to open together when we were on our way. Stretching out my arm, I reached down into the side of my boot, pulling out the envelope between my hands. Leo saw what I was doing, and moved closer to me so that we might read it together. I opened the envelope cautiously. Inside there was a letter, written on paper less worn than the envelope, but still old. I slipped out the paper that had been folded so carefully, and in opening it, found many banknotes hidden inside. On the paper there was the rounded handwriting of Marlen, familiar to both of us, while at the end there appeared an insert written by Alfredo in his spidery hand. I began to read.

> *My dearest children,*
> *As you have surely seen, inside this paper there is money. It is much, but we are sure that you will use it only when you have need, and that it will see you safely to America. Do not worry for us: Alfredo has done well in his medical career, and we have saved enough from when we were young to last us until the end of our lives. We saved this to send our Tommy to*

university, but we were never able to do this for our beloved son. Now though, we have you, who are for me and Alfredo as our own children, and we are sure that this money will much better serve you young people than us old ones. Remember always that you are always welcome in our home, and that neither I nor Alfredo could ever forget you. We hope desperately that you will have the chance to return someday to France and us and our little house, hidden away in the country. Do not forget us, we pray you.

With great affection,

Marlen DeNeri

Dearest Children,
I see that Marlen has explained everything necessary concerning the money that we have sent with you: actually, that old witch of mine has

probably said too much! I wish you well, but with great sadness, and I hope to find you back with us soon, in a France that is again free and rich. I love you both so well, with such affection.....

Alfredo DeNeri

P.S. Take care of the charm, little one...........

Finished reading the letter, I felt an immense gratitude toward the old couple that had taken us in and given us shelter and affection and compassion, and that now offered even money for our journey. I looked at Leo, who was still fixed on the letter. Realizing that I watched him, he raised his head and smiled.

"If one day I have even half of their good spirit and heart, I will be a happy man," he said in a low voice, then leaning his face toward me and kissing me with great tenderness. We drew away, and I slipped my hand inside his, feeling his skin warm and soft against mine. Folding the letter carefully as it had been and replacing it in the envelope, I held it to my heart. Meanwhile Leo took the money carefully in hand, counting it with a speed and accuracy that spoke volumes of his former life.

"You are very mathematical, aren't you?" I asked him.

"Well, my father was a businessman, and so from when I was small he taught me mathematics and economics. Then at school, I always found the mathematics one of the most interesting classes, and I intended to go to university to study economics and art, but then the war broke out, and…." he replied, dealing the banknotes into groups of higher and lower value, trying to estimate how much we would need to get through our journey.

I let him continue in peace, and pulled from the bag the book of poetry that Henri had given me. He had placed a bookmark decorated with golden thread in the book, and taking it between my fingers, I opened the book to the place he had marked. To my surprise, I saw that the pages were empty, without even numbers to mark them. I turned the pages with wonder, counting in all nearly forty. On the first page, that had been empty, there were written some lines in the tight precise script that I knew to be Henri's – the same in which was written that fateful letter that had started this journey so long ago, before Francoise and I had ever left Paris in search of him. I began to read, already feeling a deep and terrible longing for my friend Henri.

> *In this book there are many beautiful poems. I think, however, that you can write them better than any. Write. Write in these empty pages everything that comes into your mind and never forget the talent that you have. You have the gift of words. I knew it the first time that you spoke to me, the first time you read me one of your poems, the first time I saw one of your stories. Never abandon this gift of yours, and remember what I say to you. Stay well and take care, and I pray you, return to France and to us when you are able. I would like for Petit Henri to know*

who is his aunt, to know who was Francoise. Before I say goodby, and send you my best wishes, I tell you one thing that I have always wanted to say to you, but that I have never been able for fear of your response. No, do not worry! I am not about to profess my undying love for you! I only wanted to ask you for your forgiveness for all that has happened, for I know, that were it not for me, Francoise would still be alive. I have carried this weight always upon my shoulders, but I pray that you know that I have done all that I have done for the love that I had...that I have...for Francoise. She is my life. I can never love again the way that I have loved her, and I want you to know that. I am still so terribly in love with her, and the only thing that keeps me from taking my own life, to join her in the afterlife, if there is one, is the thought of Petit Henri, who is all that remains to me now. I pray you therefore: try to understand that I repent everything that I

*have caused to happen, but all the same, if
I could go back, I would do everything as
I have before, because even a few months
with Francoise is better than a lifetime
without her, and in the end, our love and
the spirit of Francoise goes on; in me, in
you....in Petit Henri.........Find a way to
come home soon......I love you...*

Henri

I lifted my eyes, full of tears again, from
this sweet page and smiled. I adored Henri, and
never once thought to blame him for the death of
Francoise, or the life that I passed without her: he
was, as was I, the sad victim of a harsh destiny;
but if I, as Henri said, could go back, I would
change nothing, for I knew surely in my heart that
Francoise lived still, in my mind and my spirit,
and if it had not been for the road that we
followed, I might never have met Leo, or Alfredo
or Marlen....and Petit Henri might never have
been born......

I looked at Leo, so intent on putting in order the banknotes and the security that they offered for our future, and smiled again, feeling a warmth inside of myself, and I kissed him. He returned my kiss, smiling and holding my hand tight in his. In that moment, I understood clearly that all that had passed was meant to be.

I turned, leaning again into the bag that we carried with us, and pulled out a pencil that I had brought along. I did not wish to forget my memories, my thoughts, my dreams. I did not know what destiny held now in store for me, but for the first time in my life, I was at peace not knowing, and I did not feel that knot in my stomach that always came just before something terrible was about to happen. And I had the charm about my neck, that I was sure would carry to us much good fortune, not only for the fact that it had served so well in the past Alfredo, but because it carried with it all of the affection of Alfredo's good heart. Smiling again, from deep inside myself, I laid my hand to the paper and began to write:

"It happened 2 January, 1938............."